Uncanny Episodes by Uncle Nafee

CUP OF TEA STUDIO

Mum & Dad, I am still trying to stop this nonsense.

First paperback published in the UK in 2024 by Cup of Tea Studio

Illustrations by Matias Muzzillo & Anna Olofsson
Cover art by Sumit Roy
Title, cover & book designed by Cup of Tea Studio

A CIP catalogue record for this book is available from the British Library.

ISBN-13: 978-1-0685384-0-7

CONTENTS

ABOUT THE AUTHOR — *THE ONLY TRUE STORY IN THIS BOOK!*

When *Uncle Nafee* (pseudonym) was in his primary school years, he stumbled across a horror book that he borrowed from a friend, and that caught his attention. His curiosity for world literature was further piqued when he rode his bike to the bookshop to buy academic books in high school. Although he got acquainted with *Arabian Nights*, fairytales, and comics in the age before he could even read. Since he couldn't read, someone had to read them to him. From that moment on, the world of his imagination began to emerge. While in high school, he spent a great deal of time reading mystery, horror, thriller, and fairytales. Writing became a fascination for him once he saw the reviews he sent to different writers in print. Seeing his name in print planted the seed of his desire to be a writer.

He began submitting amateur stories, limericks, and poems to popular magazines and newspapers, but they were never published. His desperate attempts to become a writer resulted in him penning a couple of stories based on foreign classics and getting them printed, but he had a strong desire to write something original.

One afternoon, he wrote a supernatural thriller story that changed everything. His aim was to get the story published in a famous teen magazine of his time, hoping that if they were to print the story they would do it in the upcoming issue. He received a letter from the magazine's deputy editor within a fortnight! Editor's letter was full of praise and confirmation that the story would appear in the upcoming issue. In the first few days after its publication, he received a great deal of correspondence from the readers. In a nutshell, that's how it all started. Consequently, his writings were published in a number of national literature magazines that he read regularly.

His first horror short story book, published in 2005.

In 2006 he published a thriller novella.

In 2009, he started editing a horror magazine known as *Horror Potrika.*

In 2012, established publishing firms began publishing his books.

Two horror/thriller compilations were also edited by him.

A television drama based on one of his stories aired on a television channel in 2016.

Neither his personal life nor his education had anything to do with his pursuit of literature, hence the omission. In his personal life, he described himself as a simpleton:

"There is a great deal of respect in my heart for every nation and spoken language around the world. Despite my beliefs, I have always been logical and that's why I consider every religion in the world to be an area of study for me. There will never be a book more original than the holy book Quran in my opinion and I believe the Quran is THE ultimate book. The current state of the globe is what I consider the greatest horror movie I have ever seen and predicting what will happen in the near future is the greatest horror story!" — Uncle Nafee.

Among his interests, he also has a passion for making short films.

He spends a considerable amount of his leisure time discovering the great works of others and admiring them without envy.

When he wonders 'How to be rich', the process and subsequent outcomes repel him.

He is a dreamer, yet, he always wakes up and strives to live a life filled with happiness, joy, and knowledge. He is a man fool enough to think this book will become a bestseller and bring him fame sky-high! — *Publisher.*

Acknowledgements

I have completely rewritten most of the stories from scratch, but maintained the original plot. Still, the original concepts of several stories have been reconstructed to make them more palatable to readers, and I feel this has improved the tone. In the process of editing, I included Jinns in most of these writings, while the original stories were written with ghosts, something I don't believe in! Due to the fact that I wrote most of these stories as a teenager, I tried to keep the exact same taste as when I wrote them originally. **My native language is not English, so I am certain there will be errors in this book. My apologies in advance if you encounter such errors while reading this book.** Thanks to Zakir Khandaker, Sharmin Aktar & Labonno Prova for assisting me with the initial translation from Bengali to English. I'd also like to thank Amanda Clouard for proofreading. I was also very pleased with the artwork produced by illustrator Matias Muzzillo & Anna Oloffson because they understood my instructions for each story. Using Hilal Er's beautiful handwritten alphabets, my author name has been crafted for this book. The cover was designed based on late Sumit Roy's individual elements that he had drawn for me a while ago. Having the opportunity to work with each of them individually was an exciting experience. After countless hours, days, and nights of hard work, it's finally time to see if the book yields the meaningful results I've long hoped for when it reaches the reader!

— *Uncle Nafee,* London.

A Horror Story

THE PORTRAIT

Mist covered the sky that night, making visibility nearly impossible. Even from a short distance, things were difficult to distinguish. With a chill that was almost palpable, the air was damp and silent.

An area of residential housing somewhere in the

town had a terrifyingly eerie atmosphere.

The moon was hardly visible, its faint light barely piercing through the thick fog. The wind was still, not a whisper in the air, making the fog seem to settle around everything like a blanket. Except for a few night owls, everyone seems to be asleep.

A group of sly foxes were somehow trying to sneak into the cars and searching under and above the vehicles in an effort to steal food.

A man crossing a lane very slowly, perhaps looking for an address, moved his head rapidly as he walked.

A few feet away from where he stopped, there was a house in which someone might still be awake.

Knock! Knock!

Immediately, the door was opened.

An extremely dry-looking man poked his head out to check on the visitor.

He must have been waiting for his takeout. Perhaps out of disappointment, his eyebrows appeared furrowed.

"…Apology for bothering you sir at such an inconvenient time...I am looking for Heran ma'am-Mr. Rowan's wife...." the stranger started, but before he had an opportunity to finish his sentence, the man at the door spoke up and said, "There's n-o-o way you can be alive! You must be a GHOST just showing up in the middle of the night for the sake of looking for someone!!" The man groaned, clearly an uneasy, annoyance swept over his face.

Trying to figure out where he was, the stranger was puzzled by the man's response to his inquiry. He felt unbalanced receiving such an unexpected response.

It's the same with the man.

He didn't expect a stranger in front of him this moment, looking for someone. He stared at the stranger from top to bottom, naturally irritated and assuming he knew what the stranger was going to ask, "She has moved out and is now renting an apartment elsewhere." Shaking his head up and down, he makes it clear to the stranger that he has answered his question with a full stop and wants him to leave.

"Do you have any idea where she has moved to?" As the stranger asked, his voice sounded apathetic and as if he was giving up hope. It's very foggy, things are difficult to see. In fact, even street lamps created blurred, eerie shadow effects in the darkness.

Hearing the noises, the foxes began hiding in the bushes.

The man stepped out sorting his robe and gave a quick glance to the outside, making the stranger step back a little in response, "Listen Mr. whoever, I'm sorry, I can't remember exactly at the moment, but I think it's somewhere in Church End. You seem desperate to find her…"

"I appreciate your help sir!" replied the stranger, sounding like he had fought himself hard just to hear what he wanted to hear. Then he turned around in a swift motion and left the place as quickly as he could.

A few shifty glowing eyes in the bushes indicate that those are cats or foxes, scared and ready to flee if caught.

But the stranger walk away really fast now.

An abrupt silence engulfed the atmosphere of the night as the last few minutes of nuisance began to disappear. It was as if a sudden darkness of the night struck the ground.

A look of perplexity spread across the dry-man's face as the stranger rushed away. The stranger's unbalanced situation made him think he might have to answer a few more questions. Usually, people searching for someone ask many questions until they feel they find them.

Although he was confident there would be some conversation with that stranger while he waited for his food to arrive, he found himself standing alone outside his door, with no one around, in complete silence.

He shrugged, stepped in and closed the door.

#

Heran was staring fixedly at the portrait of Sherlock Holmes on her bedroom wall.

There was a feeling of doubt in her mind that Rebaad, the artist, might have lied.

She brought this portrait from him at a spiritual art exhibition where all patients with sleep paralysis attended to have their fears painted by the artists. In their descriptions of their sleep paralysis moment, they basically try to describe what they witnessed or experienced. An artist immediately attempt to portray the scene based on what they said.

Heran had suffered from sleep paralysis for a very long time, and her doctor finally suggested she attend that event. Even if it may seem superstitious, it is not harmful to check such possibilities in order to maintain peace of mind and mental strength.

What's really interesting is that when Heran described her nightmare to Rebaad, he immediately drew that and said he could help. Basically, it was a pure portrayal of Heran's favourite detective character, Sherlock Holmes! Despite being in darkness, he was clearly visible.

Rebaad said if a Jinn possesses someone and attempts to appear in front of the victim as a fictional character, which the victim is so obsessed with, this kind of Jinn can be caged.

In spite of looking like a lifeless man who was out of his depth, Rebaad had a very confident look on his face as he gazed at Heran. Heran couldn't disbelieve him just because he said it in a way that was hard for her to disbelieve.

Did he lie about everything he said to sell the portrait?

He had assured her that on the night of fog, the painting would come to life. The night will be misty, dark, and very quiet.

A night when no one will be outside.

There will be no one awake.

There will be no sound of life at all.

The night will be very peaceful and silent.

It was in fact possible to physically see Sherlock Holmes emerging from the portrait!

But the most unusual thing Rebaad said was that if anyone happens to see Sherlock during a night of fog like this without the paralysis session, it would be an extremely rare occurrence.

"It's possible that the person isn't even alive!" This is what Rebaad said to her.

Even though it seemed absurd at the time, Heran implicitly believed it in her heart. She had bought the painting on a whim and had no explanation for what she had done, and now the idea had been bugging her for quite some time now.

Heran writes incredibly engaging ghost stories for an online streaming platform, and although she has a Masters degree in forensic science and has worked in the police force for many years, for no apparent reason, she still obsesses over paranormal things like that.

But tonight seems to be the only night that matches Rebaad's description! Heran had never seen a night like this during her wait.

Heran returned to the bed and sat down.

The steam that emanates from her still

untouched tea cup emits a hint of a wonderful aroma that engulfs the room.

There is also an open book that lies upside down on the bedside cabinet called *In the Night of Darkness*. There is a photo of Heran on the back cover.

In the room, the fresh fragrance of tea can be smelled, but Heran cannot focus on anything else. While her attention was drawn to Sherlock's portrait, she also glanced at the wall clock.

The time is 1 a.m.

Nothing whatsoever appeared to be happening at any point in time.

Heran decided that it didn't make any sense to stay up all night thinking about such a nonsense idea, especially since it was so idiotic. But this is not the case, Heran has never been awake so late without a reason. During her work life, she was usually busy doing crime scene investigation, so she isn't used to such loneliness. Her usual practice during such times is to perform both two and two four-rakat Tahajjud prayers, but she has found this difficult since becoming ill. It would be more sensible to have a good night's sleep. As the matter of fact, she must see if her husband will return home, since she is very much certain that if she goes to sleep thinking such thoughts, she will experience sleep paralysis.

She averted her gaze from the portrait and decided to text her husband.

That was when the doorbell rang.

It wasn't a surprise at all.

It must be Rowan... Heran thought to herself with a sigh of relief.

Rowan, her husband, is a forensic expert. The nature of his job, as well as the result of the hectic work schedule that he follows, he always arrives home late at night. It is possible that he will not return home in some cases.

The two used to work together. Then, Heran's health began to weaken. One day it turned out that she had a stroke and had been paralysed for several months, so she quit her job to focus only on writing and resting.

It was Rowan who first noticed Heran's extreme laziness and gradual apathy towards her responsibilities. Even on a pure sunny day, she was sleeping in her room with the curtain closed!

It is true that they were in some financial difficulties, but normally in such situations, they would perform salat more often. Heran, in particular, used to work long hours and fast almost every other week. Nowadays, she seems to be finding peace in what keeps her away from jobs and responsibilities. Such signs are known to Rowan. It is only the first step Satan takes to ruin a person's entire good deeds and bring them to their demise!

Heran put her slippers on before heading to the front door. It took her a moment to realise she had not touched her cup of tea yet.

I am going to make a cup of tea for Rowan and I'll hit mine... Heran stood up mumbling to herself.

When she opened the door, her jaw dropped.

She was surprised to find Rebaad standing there.

The artist who had drawn her Sherlock Holmes' portrait.

"Mr. Rebaad!" She beckoned him inside, "Please come on in."

Rebaad's expression of fright and apprehension was very surprising to Heran. She had not anticipated seeing him look this scared.

As soon as Rebaad entered the house, he apologised and said, "It was very difficult for me to find your address." He went on to explain, "I met your previous landlord, and he told me that you had moved to this area."

As Rebaad steps into the living room, Heran does not ask how he found her address, making Rebaad's situation easier- "I totally did not expect you to show up at such a late hour, Mr. Rebaad, but why do you look so frightened!" Said Heran.

They went into the living room.

"What makes you rush here so late at night, Mr. Rebaad? Is it the Sherlock portrait?" Heran wondered.

"We don't have much time, Mrs. Heran! We need to stop this!" As Rebaad glanced at his watch, astonished. "Go get the portrait. Please hurry!" He insisted, "Mrs Heran, I was a bit wrong. Actually, that thing has been trapped in that frame since we drew it! There are many people who cannot so accurately describe what they experience or see when they are experiencing sleep paralysis. You framed it, though! We must do something to prevent this from happening. I think we should use holy water to destroy it! There is no doubt that it would work..."

With a sigh Rebaad found himself very anxious. He is trying to locate the Sherlock Holmes frame around him.

Since everything is moving so quickly, Heran listens to Rebaad. "I'll bring it here." This was all Heran could say after experiencing Rebaad's condition.

Her mind wandered as she walked into her bedroom, pondering what had happened to Rebaad that had caused him to act in such an odd, uncanny manner.

In order to be safe, Heran decided to make a call to Rowan as a precaution.

She called him before going into the bedroom using the cordless phone in the corridor. Rowan said he would arrive in about twenty minutes.

After hanging up the phone, Heran entered the bedroom and stopped dead in her tracks!

What she saw almost made her eyes pop out of her face with shock and fright!

Sherlock Holmes was no longer pictured in the portrait!

On the wall, there was just an empty frame.

#

"Mr. Rebaad, I can't believe what just happened..." Heran's eyes were looking for Rebaad as she entered the living room.

The shock was not over yet.

She discovered that Rebaad stood perfectly still like a lifeless statue, a statue devoid of life!

His eyes are still moving in a state of dismay and is trying to say something out loud…

Heran's fear had grown to a real level now.

It was as if her heart was beating like a drum.

The statue of Rebaad looked like nothing more than a stone made object.

Her heart skipped a beat when the doorbell rang again, shattering the night's silence.

It must be Rowan, assuming second time, Heran was about to walk to the front door when… she realised she couldn't move!

The empty frame of Sherlock Holmes was in her hand.

A massive mirror frame hung right next to Heran on the living room wall.

She cannot even move her fingers or her head!

But Heran managed to look in the mirror and was shocked to see that she looked just like Rebaad.

Almost like a statue!

Heran is certain that what she feels right now is exactly like something that has no life. Without a soul, a stone statue exists only as a monument. As her ears reverberated only one thing, she remembered Rebaad's words: *It's possible that the person isn't even alive!*

The reason she can tell she is alive is that her eyes are also moving, just like Rebaad's. In colour, she smells and sees everything, without any glitches or hearing problem.

She find the feeling to be extremely uncanny and impossible to explain. Inexplicably not possible to describe.

It is only her eyes that move and what she sees that she can feel. Right now whatever she sees in the mirror isn't visible in the room!

It was precisely through the mirror that Rebaad also saw what Heran was seeing- pure Sherlock Holmes! Reading Doyle's books, Heran's imagination depicted Sherlock Homes just as this.

Rebaad can sense the immense power of that uncanny being. Despite facing many spirits before, this one paralysed him and would not let him use his hands or body.

Rebaad reminded himself that his brain and senses are still working!

A bottle of Zamzam water is open in his hand.

He appeared in a great deal of pain.

In his mind, Rebaad recited Ayatul Kurshi, The Throne Verse, which is the 255th verse in Chapter two of the Quran. The verse speaks about how nothing and nobody is regarded to be comparable to Allah. There is no question that this is one of the most remembered Quranic verses. In many cases, reciting this verse is effective in warding off Jinn.

As Rebaad recites the verses of the Ayatul Kurshi, he realises he can now use his lips and tongue! The more he delved into his mind, the louder his recitation became. There's a bounce to every word he pronounces, making the eerily quiet living room more alive and cutting through the darkness of the night!

Rebaad was finally able to use his right hand.

Through a guess, Heran saw Rebaad dump holy water on the spirit!

The entire mirror was glowing with a strange shape, which was fully engulfed in fire. Then, both witnessed Sherlock disappearing into Heran's picture frame at an incredibly quick pace...leaving the atmosphere serene.

But in a flash, the frame was on fire!

Heran's hand feels heavy and she was unable to

hold the picture frame as if someone just popped into the frame and it became heavier, extremely heated.

Heran passed out as she heard the doorbell ringing continuously for the third time, but now her husband screaming her name, "Heran! Heran!! Open the door!!!"

———

A Scary Story

THE SHOWCASE

During the early hours of a Saturday morning, Roya noticed the new tenant moving into their apartment opposite. She heard the movers and saw them carrying boxes with their belongings into the building.

Looks like a small family with just parents and a

daughter.

They can even be seen from Roya's seventh floor balcony, since their balcony is right opposite her, but on the 6th floor.

It's a beautiful morning on Roya's balcony, and she was enjoying her morning cup of tea while watching the sunrise and trying to draw it as well. She has a knack for drawing random things when she has a moment to spare, including snakes, of course! A beautiful day like today is just a typical day for her, but the sun made her draw this beautiful natural scene instead of snakes today. But it is clearly visible in that drawing that, if one pays close attention to the branches of the leaves and their shapes, they all bear a resemblance to snakes!

The block, where Roya lives, is located in the middle of a tea garden, which is a little away from the city, but still very convenient.

The area is very green and tree-filled.

Roya is always drawn to explore the neighbouring tea garden bushes, since she has heard that snakes of all kinds, including poisonous snakes, can be seen in those bushes. There is even some rumour in the fact that some crushed trees are watched over by big snakes like anacondas!

Roya still can remember when she began to love drawing snakes…

It was when her father moved to this rural tea garden that she encountered her first sighting of some people stalking a python one afternoon on their way down the trail. The snake was rescued and given to the nearby forest quarter. Before they took the python, she took a picture of it and drew her first landscape from it at home. It measured almost 13 feet long. As a result of that drawing, she won a prize at school and has never stopped drawing since then…

'E-m-m-y-e-e!'

Roya might have heard the girl's mother's voice from the balcony because she called so loudly.

Roya saw Emmy, a girl her age, running into another room.

She has very long hair that covers her entire face. It is a surprise to see how skinny and tall Emmy is, compared to Roya, a 15-year-old girl who is overweight.

It appears that Emmy had taken some 'trash' home with her, and her mother is now about to blow her mind by telling her to keep them away from her sight. After seeing this, Roya shook her head and shouted to herself, *Why am I bothering their business...* and tried to concentrate on drawing her sunrise. It is not only the aroma of her morning tea that soothes her, but it also gives her a feeling of ease and comfort as she draws, which allows her to feel more relaxed and at ease.

A few minutes later, Roya heard Emmy's voice.

With her tea cup in hand, Roya was simply unable to resist looking out at the balcony once again while taking a sip of it.

It was a struggle for Emmy to carry her things to the balcony while being yelled by her mother, but her mum also tries to help bring things up to the balcony, which was so thoughtful.

As Roya didn't want to get caught by them, she kept trying to avoid looking at their balcony as much as she could. It turns out, however, that there is a twist to the scenario!

Roya only heard one single word from Emmy's mother, and that was *Snake!*

Due to her curiosity, she tries to see what's going on between Emmy's mum and Emmy, and that's when she notices Emmy's landscape.

She was surprised to discover that Emmy has quite a few drawings that include snakes on them, which shocked her!

From this distance, Roya is clearly able to see Emmy's open art papers and is able to notice that Emmy has drawn super creepy snakes all over her art papers!

It is possible that this is the reason as to why her mother shouts at her all the time.

Roya decided to meet Emmy this afternoon!

#

Roya was unable to go to Emmy's apartment that afternoon for some reason.

The family had been in the new block for four days, but Emmy had never stepped outside the apartment since they had moved in. It was quite strange to see that happen!

There was no sign of her ever going up to the balcony after that Sunday.

The next morning, Roya decided that she would learn a little bit more about Emmy and figure out how she would go twenty-four hours cooped up inside the apartment without getting bored.

There was usually no one at home to watch Emmy since her parents were usually working. Roya heard that they both worked in a zoo (no wonder!) at the same time.

It is a holiday week, which means there won't be any school, so Roya have to wonder why they left Emmy home alone all day?

Astonished, Roya quickly rushed to Emmy's block to see what was going on.

In the morning sun, the atmosphere is pleasant. A flock of birds flew overhead. From somewhere around, some crows are calling. There are lush, green hills surrounding these tea gardens, making them seem like gardens of paradise!

Roya actually ran to Emmy's apartment and went inside. Because of her abundance of curiosity, there was no second thought in Roya's mind when she stepped into the lift and pressed the floor number 6 without any hesitation.

#

The door finally opened after Roya knocked several times.

Emmy was standing in the doorway of the room.

She had pale skin, and her body was extremely slim, which made her appear to be very thin. A wavy layer of pitch black hair covered one side of her face, which looked like snake tails. Yet she keeps moving that part of her hair quite a bit to see what's in front of her clearly.

Her eyes were sharp and cold, just like the eyes of a snake! As if she had become a snake herself just by drawing snake pictures!

Roya felt a chill run down her spine. She reminded herself that judging someone's appearance has nothing to do with being afraid!

Emmy stared curiously, smiling sharply at her.

"Assalamu Alaikum..." Roya greeted. "I'm Roya, Roya Yekub, I live in the apartment opposite yours. I think you're new here, so I came to say hello." She managed to introduce herself to Emmy.

"Oh really?" Emmy replied, smiling. "Please come in," she welcomed Roya, stepping back and opening the door wide.

"Thank you." Roya replied, as she entered the passageway.

Emmy led Roya into the living room as she closed the door behind them.

"Sorry, I didn't understand what you said at first, something like *Assala...*" While walking through the passageway, Emmy looked at Roya with interest.

"Oh! Basically, it means - *Peace be upon you.*

Every time a Muslim person meet another Muslim person exchange this greeting to each other." Roya explained.

"Interesting!" Emmy exclaimed. Her respect was evident. "I am sorry, I don't know how to answer this…"

"The opposite person usually responds by saying *Walaikum Assalam*, which means- *May peace be upon you as well.*" Roya tried to give Emmy a clear clue. But she felt a bit shy now as Emmy's name gives away the fact that she is unlikely to be a Muslim.

As one of Roya's most common habits, she practices *Salam*, the greeting. It was particularly hard for her to resist when meeting someone for the first time.

Emmy nodded her head in understanding as she stepped into the living room.

It was a moment of silence for Roya as soon as she entered the living room!

On every inch of the wall, there were countless sketches of snakes all over it! In fact, the sketches were so real that the snakes appeared to be alive in them.

The thought struck Roya that all the snakes in

the world must be gathered in one place.

As Emmy asked Roya to take a seat, she took a seat as well and introduced herself, "I am Emmy. That is all my work. I drew all those snake pictures."

Roya was full of praise as Emmy exclaimed, "It's so amazing! They're really beautiful," she said in awe.

"It is very kind of you Roya, thanks. I heard you also draw. That is awesome. I wanted to meet you, but I've been extremely busy lately, so I didn't have time to call you." Emmy says.

"It's okay, I understand. But how you can spend the entire day here?" Roya asked. "There has never been a time when I have seen you leave your apartment!"

A mysterious smile spread across Emmy's face and she said, "Well, my parents have forbidden me to go out. But now that you've come I have a friend!"

Trying to make herself as comfortable as possible, Roya smiled and began to relax.

Then she pulled out a few sketches of imaginary snakes from her bag so she could give them to Emmy.

Roya noticed that Emmy shivered a little bit as she was doing so.

But as quickly as she could, Emmy controlled herself and thanked Roya for the gift. She said, “These are completely new to my collection,” and added, “let’s go into my room to see what I have there.”

Roya was a bit indecisive, but Emmy took her hand and pulled her up, “Come on, didn’t we just become friends?”

Roya followed Emmy to her room rather against her will. There are just so many uncanny situations accumulating around her head that she cannot comprehend!

There was a great shock waiting for her.

She felt the hair on her neck bristle with fear and her heart started pounding as she tried to calm herself.

Throughout the room were glass showcases with thousands of snakes displayed inside.

Alive, repulsive and fearsome!

With a great fear, Roya stepped back and turned around to leave the room.

As she looked around, she realised that Emmy was no longer there.

There was even no sign of the door she had just walked through!

Roya screamed out Emmy's name over and over again but her voice was drowned out by the hissing of thousands of snakes!

Petrified, Roya saw that for no apparent reason the shelves had suddenly started to crash to the ground.

And as the glass cages broke, the snakes came out into the open!

Roya froze in her tracks.

Her throat went dry.

The snakes advanced towards her like angel of death!

She felt that she was very soon going to die.

She succumbed to her fear and closed her eyes, to helplessly await their poisonous bites!

#

The first thing Roya felt was the warmth of a breath on her neck, and then she felt the hand of someone touch her.

In an instant, her senses were suddenly awakened, and opening her eyes, she saw Emmy smiling at her, holding a cup of tea in her hand.

Emmy handed Roya the cup of tea.

"Are you feeling okay?" Emmy asked if Roya was okay after observing her condition, "You can see my study room where I also draw things. My mum said I could use the balcony, but I couldn't bear the wind outside, so I chose the study room instead."

"Yes, of course!" Roya strove to keep herself steady and fit as she dealt with the situation. The situation she was in was extremely disturbing. There was something unsettling and uncanny about it.

Nothing could possibly be more real than this!

It cannot be unreal at all!

As Roya looked back at the room, she had another shock!

There was no showcase at all.

Not a single trace.

Emmy's room was just like a typical girl's bedroom.

Neat and clean and not a single sketch of a snake hanging anywhere!

#

Roya spent the rest of her time at Emmy's apartment completely dumbfounded.

Emmy showed her numerous pictures of snakes, videos and CDs, dresses and books, but Roya found it difficult to pay attention. Finally she said goodbye to Emmy and went home.

She felt hypnotised, as if she were caught up in some kind of hoax.

Roya is still shocked by what she saw at Emmy's house. Her gaze fell on the kitchen bin for a moment as she walked through the passageway saying goodbye. It was a lot of dried, broken bones that she saw! That's all there is! As she knows, Jinns love decaying bones!

She was not even sure how she had got home, but once there she went straight to the bathroom, feeling sick.

What had happened seemed so real that she couldn't keep it out of her mind. A hallucination would have made more sense…

Suddenly Roya felt a sharp pain on her ankle.

As she looked down to see what was causing this agonising pain, her eyes became riveted on what she saw.

Both her legs had swollen up and were slowly turning blue.

Poison was spreading throughout her body!

Then Roya understood.

Especially when she realised that her entire skin had been bitten!

A Chilling Horror

THE MONA LISA

It took Leonardo da Vinci almost three to four years to draw the Mona Lisa portrait, but Habib Molla managed to do it in just three days!

There's nothing surprising about that. In drawing Mona Lisa, Habib Molla used the sfumato technique in the same way that Vinci did. His attention to detail was remarkable, and even though he drew it in such a short period of time, the details were still very original. It would thus pass for an original, except for someone with very experienced eyes. It turned out to be just as beautiful and alive as the original!

When experienced artists are able to create paintings using only a few pencil strokes, then it isn't so difficult for them to copy an already existing portrait when they are skilled enough to do so. To begin with, all they need to do is make sure that the primary sketch is drawn correctly, and then to colour it is merely a matter of time and imagination.

Habib Molla fits the bill as well, because he's very skilled and professional at what he does.

The only thing he craves when concentrating on drawing is tea. It took him almost 100 cups of tea to finish drawing the Mona Lisa. A hot, steamy, and fresh cup of tea with a little sugar is just what he needs to finish coping any original art piece. When he goes to the local tea shop, he always orders a spicy, fragrant tea, and the boy there always gives him a full flask. Habib even gets it delivered to him if he gives them a call and leaves some tips for the boy who is delivering it.

It was a beautiful sunny Sunday, and the weather couldn't have been more perfect.

With his freshly ordered tea in hand, Habib Molla felt refreshed. He took a sip from his half finished cup of tea. Mona Lisa was painted in the centre of the wall of the bedroom, right in the middle of the bed. There were many other drawings on the wall, but all of them were underneath this new masterpiece.

Habib scrutinised his painting closely while sipping his steamy tea. He wanted to make sure that the drawing had no flaws. The mysterious smile, the mesmerising gaze, everything seemed spot on, as if Leonardo da Vinci himself had drawn a revised version of the Mona Lisa!

Habib Molla was impressed with his 'own' work!

It has been a month since he drew the old design, but he never felt the urge to draw anything on top of it. His feelings were a little uncanny actually, as he wondered whether this painting was causing him to become obsessed with it.

A painting did not usually stay with him for longer than a week, but the Mona Lisa was an exception. Habib Molla had the feeling that erasing the drawing would not be the right thing to do for some uncanny reason. Since he's leaving the house this afternoon anyway, it wouldn't make sense to erase anything at the last minute for the sake of being tidy.

Habib Molla moves every other month from one place to another. This is how he works. In no way could he stay in one place for longer than three months at a time. Fortunately, his landlords weren't too bothered by his portraits.

Now, whether or not he should leave the Mona Lisa portrait as a gift to the house was Habib's dilemma. He was a little bugged that it wasn't his original work. But he ultimately decided to leave it to the landlord's discretion.

Habib Molla stood up holding his cup of tea.

He pushed the old stool aside with his foot.

The bedroom, which was full of his belongings just yesterday, was now empty except for his drawings on the wall. He had already sent his furniture and everything else to his new place.

Now is the time to say goodbye to this place.

While Habib Molla gazes out the window, he observes the beauty of nature around him.

The green tea gardens outside are like carpets of heaven. It blows a gentle breeze. There's something different about it.

Habib's mind cannot explain why he is feeling so uncanny today; he has never really had the chance to look around anywhere he lived or stayed before.

A few seconds later, Habib pulled his head out of the scene and sipped his tea as quickly as he could.

His mind keeps shifting to make a quick move because this place is starting to get to be too much for him right now.

He isn't sure if it's emotional, uncanny, or just his inability to comprehend what's going on.

Habib Molla was almost out of the room, he turned back for a final look at the painting and stopped dead in his tracks!

As he stared into the distance, a huge frown appeared on his forehead along with a look of shock in his eyes.

He struggled to balance, the strength of his knees began to deteriorate.

It was as if his knees were shaking!

Habib Molla was awestruck, terrified, frightened

and petrified when he realised that the smile on the lips of the Mona Lisa had disappeared!

#

"Oh, what an incredible painting, Aunty!" Raihan exclaimed, though his voice was tinged with disappointment, "I would have taken it if it was in a frame."

The landlady said, "That's the only reason I'm not painting the walls. Everyone who lived here before you praised the portrait same way."

The landlady and her tenant Raihan were chatting in front of the painting of the Mona Lisa.

Having lived there for two months, Raihan was moving out that day. He was truly obsessed with this painting.

He learned that an artist named Habib Molla had painted the portrait almost a year ago, but it remained as good as new.

It had all been well maintained by the tenants who lived there.

"Aunty, I wish I could meet Mr. Habib! He's such a genius!" His eyes then shifted to the landlady's embarrassment.

The look on her face was rather startling.

As Raihan is about to leave, this seems like the perfect time to bring up this humour and justify the fact.

Habib Molla's dead body was found in an eerie state, on the floor. There was nothing abnormal about his body, except for his lips! There was nothing under his nose and his eyes were wide open. It was as if he had never had a mouth before!

It is actually not an appropriate idea for landlords to disclose anything about the previous tenant to their new tenant. Who will rent then? A matter like this cannot be covered up, especially when something terrible happens and people end up shivering over it.

"It was a terrible accident! Mr. Habib had passed away..." said the landlady. "It's been a while, but he died the day he was about to move. When we found him, he was unconscious on the floor. He was taken to the hospital and..."

There is no doubt that she doesn't want to reveal the exact truth for fear of people not renting this place in the future.

"Oh no!" Raihan attempts to make the situation little comfortable, "I thought I'd ask Mr. Habib to draw me!"

The landlady giggled, "Isn't that a bit weird?" she joked, as she shook her head at her momentary awkwardness. As if in response to each other, they burst into laughter. Despite the fact that they were laughing, Raihan believes that the landlady was annoyed by the joke. Possibly she's saying in her mind that what if the same thing happen to him!

Yes, what if...

Raihan's apprehension intrigued him and he tried to dismiss this ominous idea from his thoughts.

"All right, Aunty, I'll go now." Raihan said, hoisting his backpack onto his shoulder. He picked up the heavy luggage and carried it to the door.

"Farewell, son..." Landlady replied, as if she feared something terrible might happen to him, "May Allah bless you."

Raihan didn't pay much attention to this valediction, but as he left, he glanced at the portrait one last time. To his surprise, the smile on Mona Lisa's lips was no longer there!

A Psychological Horror

SERVANTS OF THE VILLA

Afia Villa is located in a charming tea garden far from the town.

Its entire structure is built on one large hilly portion where there are a variety of fruit trees, tea bushes, and many other kinds of plants, most of which are flowers. The air is filled with flowers' sweet scent and birds' chirping. It's a place that's truly one of a kind.

Several of the neighbouring houses can be seen from the balconies, but they are too far away from the villa and not that close. The town centre is about ten minutes away by car from the villa.

The owners of the villa, Anis Chowdhury and Dina Chowdhury, lived there with their three servants- driver Amin, maid Munia, and caretaker Hakim.

This story revolves around Dina Chowdhury, who is the main character in the story. Since the story begins and ends through her, it makes sense that she is the central character. So let's get to know her a little better.

Despite the fact that Dina is only thirty years old, appears more like an older woman. She had a gloomy, frustrated face. Apart from her husband, no one else in the house could stand her. This is not because she is rude to anyone, or that she behaves in an unfriendly manner. In fact, she is quite the opposite. There's no doubt that she's a very generous person and a true innocent minded woman. As for her, she is constantly in a state of confusion, wondering why her servants are so rude to her!

Everyone around her ignores her all the time.

One afternoon, for instance, she was sitting in front of the television watching a show with Munia standing beside her, completely absorbed in whatever they were watching together. In the case if Dina requested Munia to make tea for them both, Munia wouldn't even bother to look at her; instead, she would just take the remote, turn up the TV volume, and simply ignore her!

This behaviour demonstrates Munia's lack of respect for Dina, and it also reinforces the power dynamic between them. By turning up the volume of the TV, Munia is silently asserting her dominance and silencing Dina.

In another instance, similarly, when Dina had to go out on an occasion and she asked their driver Amin to get the car out for her, Amin replied that he was taking a rest, and therefore, he would not be able to do that for her!

Hakim, caretaker, was no exception either.

If he was asked to post a letter for her, he would take it but never let her know if he had actually posted it or not!

These are very common situations that Dina

encounters in her everyday life. But what's surprising is that none of these things seem to affect Dina in any way. It had been almost eight years since she had come to live at Afia Villa and in all those years she had never raised her voice to any of her servants.

Dina had a habit of going and doing things herself if the maid wouldn't do them. She would typically drive the car herself instead of bothering the driver, in order to avoid any hassle on her part. There was never a time when she expressed anger towards her servants in any way. Not only that, but Dina Chowdhury felt certain that if her husband found out about all her servants' misbehaviour, he would lock them up for their whole lives. This is why she never brought it up to him. There is nowhere for these people to go, as far as she knows. If Anis ever realises this, their lives will be in hell. In other words, he would send them to the hospital first.

Despite all of this, Dina Chowdhury did not tell her husband anything about any of this. She maintained a busy schedule with her writing and other activities that kept her calm. Whenever she needed to send letters, she would wait until she had a few and then send them all at the same time when she went out shopping during the day.

That's how her days went by.

It could have been worse, but she was always able to hide the sadness on her face no matter how bad the situation was. It was difficult for her, but her days were spent alone. As a matter of fact, even though she has no problem with Anis being busy with his work and staying outside all the time, she often finds herself alone, and wants to make the villa a little more lively and crowded, as a result, it is sometimes nice to see people walking around, which lessens her loneliness.

Every single time the servants gathered together, they used to chitchat among themselves. It was not uncommon for them to spend hours sitting on the lawn and talking to each other. There was no one like them in Dina's life to talk to her in such a manner. Despite this, she was relieved to be relieved from the burden of having to live alone in such a big house for the time being. This doesn't mean that she did not sometimes feel the urge to ask them if they all felt hated for her, and if so, why did they feel that way and what made them feel that way?

But she didn't ask. She let them have their own time as they pleased.

Anis Chowdhury's mother was Afia Begum. His father's name was Abed Chowdhury. The villa used to be where Anis Chowdhury's parents lived, but they passed away a long time ago. Anis named the house after his mother - *Afia Villa.*

As of that time, when his parents were alive, Anis had successfully begun his entrepreneurial career and used to live in another city. It was his career that forced him to move away from his parents.

Then, he lost both his parents, and ever since, he has never been able to overcome himself being so self-centred, and he has never lived anywhere else for more than a week if his business requires him to do so. For the sake of keeping their villa alive, he hired Amin, Munia, and Hakim as servants to work at the villa.

It was expected of him, as an orphan, that he would run a small business so that he could survive and take care of the villa that his parents had left him. But upon seeing that he had already set up thousands of people who are sustaining their lives from the business he ran, he found that it wasn't easy to let go of things so easily with so many people dependent on it. As a result, he couldn't adhere to his emotions. His mind gradually started moving on, and it also helps him to avoid thinking about his parents and getting emotional as much as possible.

At the beginning, Anis wasn't interested in getting married.

There was no doubt that he was a successful businessman. His life was extremely busy most of the time, and he knew this would complicate his marriage.

Amin, Hakim, and Munia were his three servants who had to take care of all the chores that had to be done on a daily basis at the villa. Yet, in spite of the fact that they were the ones who begged him to get married and somehow convinced him to do so. It was Anis' perspective that these people were the only ones left on earth able to care for him in any way. This is the only few people to whom he has always believed that he can always count on to never leave him alone in life. It was normal for him to leave the entire villa to them while on a business trip. He never felt concerned about leaving it all to them during those trips. Ultimately, he decided to get married when all of them urged him to do so, and he was happy that he did.

As much as he loved his wife, Anis always tried his best to keep Dina happy and when he did, he realised he didn't even need to strain hard to keep her happy.

When Dina got married to Anis, she was already a successful writer and was fully aware of Anis's busy lifestyle.

The problem Anis encountered was that this woman was far too honest and incredibly simple to handle that he could not handle it!

Most people tend to think that the wives of millionaires are a bit shrewish and bossy, sometimes even dominating their own husbands when it comes to their own interests. Dina Chowdhury was one of those rare exceptions to the rule. According to Anis, they are a super happy couple, full of a lot of other people's love and working hard to be the best at what they do. There has never been any complaint or issue that Dina brought up with him about anything, and as far as Anis knows, she seems to be just fine with her marital life. There are times when she does seem quite down, but it could be because of the job that she has. The last time her book was released, it sold over ten million copies! There must be so much she is doing to make sure her book sells so well.

As the old saying goes, the truth doesn't stay hidden for long, so it is best not to try to hide it. Dina cannot disclose anything on her own, but when someone does good for others, nature also has a responsibility to play!

One day, Anis rang home.

Dina was in the middle of writing a story at the time.

Away from the telephone.

They had a cordless telephone in her room, as well as a wired phone downstair's.

Hakim probably took the call.

He was told that Anis won't be home.

The result of this was that Dina would not be eating that night. No matter how late Anis returned from work, back in all the years of their marriage, Dina never had dinner without her husband.

There is no doubt in Dina's mind that no one will prepare dinner for her. The chances are that Dina will not be able to find anything to eat in the kitchen, even if she decides to eat a snack. But that is not the case, she is just unaccustomed to Anis being absent when it is out of Anis' business hours.

But it's ok, she gets it.

She always gets lost in her writing for long periods of time without even realising how much time is passing.

As the clock ticked down, taking a look left-right; Dina saw she had made flasks of tea earlier. Applauding herself, in the midst of her writing, Dina plunged once more into her work.

#

It was just after midnight when Anis returned without warning.

Dina was still deep in her writing and she didn't even notice that Anis approached her and smiled at her without disturbing her writing.

Anis could tell by looking at Dina that she hadn't eaten lunch or dinner for sure.

The servants were asleep. But, as soon as they heard the sound of movement at home, they were shocked to notice Anis's presence as if they had just seen a ghost for the very first time!

Since Anis always calls them first, no one expected him to return like this .

But Anis isn't sure why they were scared!

Anis wasn't bothered by these at all.

But neither Dina's study room nor the kitchen have any sign that she ate her dinner or that food was prepared for her. And this is something that bothers Anis.

It's not unusual for Dina to stay in her room writing for the most part of the time, and sometimes they end up eating dinner at the very late hours of the night especially when Anis comes home late. When this happens, the maids typically prepare slightly different dishes and other types of food so that everyone can enjoy them with curiosity.

There was something that Anis felt didn't seem right about the situation.

Dina, on the other hand, realised that Anis was back, taking a shower. It made her so happy. Her face, however, changed as she saw Munia, Hakim, and Amin staring at her with fear, Dina's face filled with mercy. They seem to believe that they have been caught by Anis and that if Dina does not save them, then something horrible is going to happen to them.

Dina tried to soothe the servants by telling them, "You can tell him that I asked for something very light to be cooked for my dinner, just some spinach and steam rice."

A sense of relief was felt by the frightened servants. They started preparing food for the couple and setting the table.

Anis came down into the dining room and didn't say a word. He sat down with Dina and since he had asked no one if she had dinner or not, Dina decided to eat with him without making things more uncomfortable.

The dinner has been served to both of them.

Seeing the fear in the faces of Hakim, Amin, and Munia, it is clear that Anis has something on his mind right now, because they are all looking at each other with worries in their eyes...

#

The dinner was over, and Dina and Anis returned to their room to rest.

Anis asked Dina to sit next to him on the bed so that he could talk to her.

The whole thing has made Dina somewhat concerned as she somehow feels that if Anis asks her about the servants then she'll be unable to lie about anything. She is not sure whether there is any other way for her to avoid lying.

"Tell me something truthfully," Anis finally asked. "Having lived with me in this house for all these years, have there ever been any moments where you felt unhappy?" He looked at her piercingly.

The only thing Dina could do was smile at her husband. It seemed that Anis wasn't up for enigmas on this particular moment. He realises that Dina is hiding something from him. Anis had to ask her quite angrily, "answer me!"

As Dina saw how her husband showed a sudden change in mood, she was not surprised. There was no way she would be able to fail to understand at the moment why he was getting to be so angry.

"I don't know what you think of me, but I'm not stupid." Observing Dina carefully, Anis said. "You've never told me if there are any problems or if you need anything. I know there is something going on that you are trying to hide from me Dina. You're acting differently now than you should, I expect you to react. Why are you like this?"

Anis arose from the bed and walked around the

room.

"There is a simple, childlike nature to your behaviour that never ceases to amaze me, but that does not mean that you should always act in a civil or courteous manner to others. What was it like when I returned home tonight and you, the mistress of the house, was awake hungry while those idiots slept? I was really humiliated by what I saw. I didn't expect you to be so stupid."

Dina still remained silent.

At that moment, she was aware that the situation was not going to be comforted by her in any way. She knew her husband.

In the midst of walking around the room, Anis stopped talking and began gripping the armchair so tightly as he stood there with anger in his eyes.

"There is just no way we can be so generous when it comes to tolerance Dina, I'm afraid." Anis looking much calmer, as he says. Walking back to Dina, he sat in front of her with his legs folded. "When it comes to tolerating someone, being considerate is nothing to get upset about. However, if it doesn't result in the person feeling guilty or making the person understand precisely what they are doing in the wrong direction, then you should not let that happen."

There is no need for Dina to respond, because Anis is sure that she understands what he means. Her understanding of what Anis was trying to convey was crystal clear to Dina.

After a while, Anis went to the bed without saying anything further, and fell asleep.

Dina didn't say anything either. She sat there motionless, watching her husband sleep.

Throughout everything Anis had said, she knew she had been punched to the gut perfectly.

In an instant, Dina felt a sudden surge of strength deep in the centre of her being.

There was something changing inside of her that she could feel.

It was as if she had a wave of power flowing through every fibre of her body!

It felt as if she wasn't the usual Dina anymore.

There was a cold sweat forming on her forehead as she started shivering.

Her gaze was drawn to the wall clock on the

wall.

It was 3 o'clock.

There was an uncanny atmosphere in the room.

#

That night, the moon was full in the sky.

Stars were shining brightly in the night sky.

Although much of the area was filled with moonlight, there were also some places where it was dark, making it harder to see things clearly through the thick bushy, dense forest in the valley.

It was in such a location that the Afia villa was located. In many angles, Afia villa lacks the beauty of the moonlight.

Dina turned off the lights in her bedroom. That room wasn't illuminated by the moonlight at all.

Anis was still fast asleep.

Dina wandered out of the room without making any sound. The darkness seemed to be the source of power that she was experiencing, but she had no idea why, or how it could be like that.

Some uncanny and incomprehensible force was working inside her.

#

Throughout the valley, there was a sense of silence.

There was not even a sound of a cricket to be heard.

The valley under the deemy moonlight seemed to have a mysterious aura about it, as if it was some kind of place that was buried deep inside the earth.

In the back garden of Afia Villa, there was three deep pit that had been dug, crammed with three corpses that were stuffed into it.

One of the corpses was of a female and the other two male.

Sweat was dripping down Anis' forehead as he was struggling to keep his forehead dry. With the palm of his hand, he was repeatedly wiping away the sweat from his brow. The cotton-made robe he was wearing was drenched with sweat although he wasn't aware of it. He was filling the graves with soil like an insane person, burying corpses underneath.

A hungry fox let out a bloodcurdling shriek that echoed through the mountains before fading into silence.

Anis Chowdhury looked up at the window of his bedroom.

As he gazed at his wife standing there in the darkness of the room, he felt something uncanny.

Sometimes Anis wonders if Dina could control herself if he ever made her upset!

It wasn't long before, but right after their marriage, Dina became possessed by a jinn. Her jinn forced her to commit dangerous acts if someone disrespected her favours or made her upset. Anis took care of it as soon as it came to his attention. In their solution, they found that if Dina stayed calm in any situation, then nothing harmful would happen to her or the jinn could not force her into harmful behaviour.

They found it to be much harder than they expected! It seems as if they live in an impossible world.

It was Dina's diagnosis that led them to realise that they themselves, the humans, were more dangerous than Jinn! There is just no desire among people to be grateful to God. The moment someone gets out of their harsh situation and begins living a better life, their mind starts looking for more and they start becoming more greedy as a result.

The only thing Anis wanted to accomplish was to get Dina to teach a lesson to their servants for their actions. But he didn't realise that it would be this much!

Dina's eyes were fixed on him as he waved.

She glanced out of the window and shook her head slightly as well.

Her attention was drawn to the graves that Anis rigged for all three servants.

But tiredness gripped her.

There was blood dripping from the knife she was holding!

She is now experiencing flashbacks that are gradually being erased from her mind.

The first attack she made on Munia was ear-splitting. Then it was so easy for her to attack Amin and Hakim together with Anis down the trail.

Running to save their lives was their only option.

It was Anis who shot both of them.

Almost a year has passed since she has not been

able to complete her manuscript due to these servants' interception. It will still be a mystery to her why those people used to annoy her so much even though she was so nice to them and never behaved bossily!

There's no doubt tomorrow will be a fresh day for Dina to finish her new manuscript all at once!

A Ghost Story

DR. MINAR'S STRANGE MUSEUM

"You made a huge mistake!" The stranger sitting next to Dr. Minar made the comment. The jolt of the car and the flash of electricity seem to have overcome him. He had been drenched from head to toe. "To be honest, you shouldn't have ventured out in this weather." He said with a smile.

It was a very windy and stormy night in Raynagar and Dr. Minar was driving very carefully while flashes of lightning and stormy winds increased in frequency and recurrence and he was considering the safety as he drove.

Dr. Minar is frustrated that the stranger isn't wrong.

While speeding up the wiper on the windshield, he shoots back, "You probably would've become dead by now if I hadn't driven by this road at this hour. This must have been good luck for you."

"There is no doubt in my mind that it's true! I am grateful to the almighty for sending you to rescue me." the stranger said.

In a flash, Dr. Minar noticed that the stranger was really thankful for God's saving him. He finds him very childlike in his appearance and in his manner of speaking.

It sounds like the stranger isn't a fully grown man at all when he speaks.

There is something about the man's age that makes it seem as if he is Dr. Minar's grandson.

There is no sign of a man in this body, but rather

a child who popped into him just like a spout of water.

"I was wondering where you were going. Even in the daytime, it's impossible to imagine anyone walking along that road in such weather! And you left on foot, alone! What's your name?" As Dr. Minar focused on the road, he asked.

"I know sir! Anyway, my name is Riku. Have you ever come across Arindam Chowdhury, the owner of the tea garden of East Raynagar, before? I wonder if you are familiar with him. I am his son..."

Crrrrrraaaaaach!!!

In a matter of seconds, the car came to a sudden halt.

As it skidded on the wet road, it caused a great shake.

They both inside experienced a hard bump for the sudden brake. There was a cupholder in the centre console of the car where Dr. Minar's tea was perched in a lidded cup.

Maybe the lid wasn't attached properly. A lot of tea spilled out of the mug with great shaking.

Dr. Minar Chowdhury scrutinised his fellow passenger with eyes popping out, "Oh dear Lord!" he said with a trembling voice.

"I apologise, sir, but what makes you so shocked?" Riku asked with such an innocent tone and wonder in his voice. The car was engulfed in a dark, oppressive silence for a few seconds, despite the rain and the thunderstorm rumbling outside.

Dr. Minar took a few seconds to get his bearings, after which he began to think clearly. Taking a look around and trying to ascertain whether everything in front of him is real.

"Are you saying Mr. Arindam, who passed away almost twenty years ago?" Dr. Minar sat straight in his seat, staring at the person who literally looks like he doesn't know what's going on around him.

"Surely you are right, sir..." Confirmed Riku, but something caught his attention. "Wait!" He rebuked. "My apologies! What did you just say? Who passed away?"

Mr. Minar's jaw dropped.

Riku seems to have no clue what he has just said, and he seems to be in total disbelief. There must be some misunderstanding going on here.

Dr. Minar restarted the car and then said, "Well, forget it." He went on to say, "What were you doing out there in the storm?"

"I can understand why you were so surprised when you saw me in such a situation. In fact, I have been looking for my house since this afternoon..." Said Riku, pulling his backpack from behind while he was explaining.

Observing Riku now, Dr. Minar notices he is dressed in a school uniform!

"What... That is insane..." He replied to Riku with a confused tone in his voice.

"Yes, I know. This is terrible!" Riku pleaded with Dr. Minar to believe him. He said, "I have been searching for this house very hard."

It is hard to believe that Dr. Minar is almost 70 years old. Even so, he is still able to see things quite clearly. There is no doubt that Dr. Minar appears older than he actually is due to his skinny skin and his impossibly white hair, but even with the age he is currently facing, he still has the strength and health in his body. Despite the full white beard, moustache, and white hair that make him look old, it seems the skin has not yet wrinkled.

Turning on the headboard light in the car, Dr. Minar glanced over at Riku.

Riku appears real, very real!

He found the inside of the car situation to be much more uncanny at this very moment than the outside situation.

"Honestly, there is no way I am going to be able to understand any of what you are saying." Turning off the headboard lights, Dr. Minar said. "We are already quite far from your house. We have to just go over to my cottage and see what I can do for you. I will be more than happy to help you. The condition of my health has deteriorated quite a bit now!"

"It is fine with me if you drop me back late. Please take your time. I'm sure my dad won't mind at all. If you could just tell him that I got lost, that would be great." The appearance of Riku right now resembles that of a lost child who was rescued by someone.

Dr. Minar focused his attention on the road and pressed the accelerators. There's nothing he wants more than to get home as quickly as possible!

#

Raynagar isn't a small place. It has been a remote tea estate for hundreds of years.

Nowadays, almost no one lives within or near this area. The trails are always deserted on a normal day. Few people can be seen walking along the path. But in the darkness of the night, there are literally no people on the trails other than a few forest rangers who drive around in jeeps in the vicinity of the trails.

The estate slowly turned into a ghostly place as dust settled in. No electricity, no lamps, nothing. The only light people have are candlelights! There is no better night for a hot cup of smoky tea than one during which thunderclouds, heavy rain, and fierce winds rage!

On the top of a small hill, which was covered in trees, the residence of Dr. Minar was nestled amongst the greenery, overlooking a large expanse of grasslands.

It's a small cottage.

In the darkness of the night, the candlelight struggles to remain alive despite the windy air that hovers over the cottage and is engulfing it in a strange sense.

Dr. Minar's strange museum, which is displayed on the wall of his drawing room, caught Riku's attention while he stood there looking at it.

In a number of glass bottles whose lids have been sufficiently secured by ropes, strange humanoid smoky figures can be seen inside, which appear to be potent in their fumes and smoke. There are a couple notes underneath each bottle that explain what it contains. As it seems, each bottle has the souls of the dead in it!

There is a bottle where Riku's eyes have been stuck for quite some time.

The level underneath that bottle says- *Arindam Chowdhury & Family, 1943-1985.*

There are approximately 5 to 7 smoky shapes inside this bottle that are reminiscent of the faces of people that belong to a family.

As Riku looks at the bottle, he sees a number of familiar faces, caged and appears to be the death soul of people he knew!

#

There is something Dr. Minar was looking for in the next room.

He was untangling old newspapers to find something. It is only a torch that he uses to light the papers as he does not have any candles left to use. From there, he could see Riku clearly.

There is no doubt that Riku's body resembles that of a child, but his head resembles that of a man of sufficient age, and his body resembles a combination of these two forms. Due to Riku's eyes being fixed on something on the wall, it became impossible to see Riku's face from where Dr. Minar is standing.

Dr. Minar finally found what he had been searching for.

A photo of a lost child was published in a news article. As of today, 11th of October 1998, it is a Monday. But the news that was published in that newspaper dates back to the 16th of February 1960, saying Riku Chowdhury, who is 11, has not come back home since Friday after school. He was wearing the uniform he had been wearing to school and was carrying his black school bag with him.

Almost 38 years old news! There has never been any trace of Riku.

This is perhaps the same Riku who lost nearly 38 years ago, when he was only 11 years old! In fact, even by looking at the photo, it is very easy to tell that it is the same person. Little Riku, whose soul grows over time, but his face remains the same!

It is not the intention of Dr. Minar to determine the causes behind the events that unfold in a person's life. Instead, he simply is concerned with finding lost souls and doing whatever it takes to ensure that they make their final departure and are free of pain and suffering. Having worked for many years rescuing lost souls, he is now able to predict what might happen to a soul based on their past.

Dr. Minar glances over to the other room just to be sure what Riku is doing.

Through the window, a brighter light flashed and brightened Riku's existence. There is no movement on his part.

Immediately after taking out his tape recorder, Dr. Minar began recording some notes very quickly:

"The time is 11 p.m. and it is Sunday, 11th of October, 1998. It seems as though Riku was on the way home from school when he saw something in the bush and as a curious child, he may have wandered into the bush to learn more about what he saw..." Dr. Minar pauses for a moment.

He dug deep into his thoughts for some reason. Trying to come up with a reasonable guess. Continuing to press the record button, he said: *"Could Riku have been bitten by a snake and got lost in some bush-covered deep pit? It is clear to me that Riku has a few snake bites on his left hand, some of which are on his neck as well..."* Once again, he paused the tape recorder.

In order to make sure he was not mistaken, Dr. Minar needed to double check one last thing!

#

There was only one candlelight in the room, which cast shadows on the objects in the room, which made the room look eerie.

The weather outside seems to have become a bit less tumultuous, the storm was subsiding and raindrops make a smooth sound in the silence as they fall.

An uncanny atmosphere permeates the cottage.

Except for the noise of the wind and light rain, there was no other sound.

Riku was not alone.

The souls of everyone else who had suffered an untimely death in the neighbourhood were standing next to him, including his own family. None of them had a shadow because dead people don't have shadows.

Dr. Minar, an eminent historian who collects dead spirits in small bottles and keeps them in his museum, noticed Riku's shadow hitting the opposite wall of candlelight! With shock, he also noticed that there was no visible shape on the floor or on the walls of his own body…

A Creepy Story

COFFIN NUMBER FIVE

The Ghosts is a popular weekly horror magazine I edit and publish. Every issue contains ten short horror stories with very dark and spooky illustrations. Since the rest of the collaborators take my instructions remotely, I am the only one who does the office work every day.

Occasionally, another person comes to help me for a few hours.

There isn't much distance between my home and my office. On a daily basis, I walk around twenty minutes to and from the office and home, so I spend a total of forty to fifthly minutes walking. It's the only time I walk, since otherwise I spend the entire day at my office desk reading and editing submissions.

Today is my day off.

It's Friday, and it's raining outside.

Following Jummah prayer, I usually have lunch later and finish reciting the Quran. The feeling struck me when I had finished reciting the Quran for an hour that I should go to the office to see if there was any mail that I needed to take care of! Hence, I prepare a cup of very hot tea for myself. When it's raining outside, I don't even step out without my lidded cup of tea in my hand.

At the time I arrived at my office, it was 4 p.m. in the afternoon.

On the entrance gate, there are all letter boxes. The only posts I see are from readers. Having taken all of them with me, I entered the office in a bad mood.

It has been a long time since Haydar posted anything, so I was expecting something from him. I cannot believe it has been six or seven weeks already! The letters I received from readers must have been triggered by their complaints about Haydar's absence from the Ghosts for almost 6-7 issues.

And yes, I was right.

Readers began sending us all kinds of questions. They wanted to know what was going on. It was the same with me! I wanted to know what was happening too!

Unfortunately, the problem was that we were unable to get in touch with Hayder for a longer period of time. Mails posted to him bounced back, his cell phone was turned off, and his landline had been disconnected. The magazines that have been sent to him by post have also been returned to office.

This unusual situation perplexed me greatly.

The magazine has been published for over a year and a half now, and Hayder has been a regular contributor since the beginning. As I had never failed to pay him on time, he was never late in sending in new stories. So I couldn't understand why he disappeared all of a sudden. The situation couldn't be left to stand by, so I decided to examine it.

Taking advantage of the rainy day, I set off for Hayder's house.

There are about 23 miles between me and his residence, which is not too far from me in terms of distance, so that isn't too lengthy for me to drive.

While sipping on my cup of tea, I truly enjoy driving.

Haydar has always lived in Mirza Jungle, where his family has roots. The house they live in is huge. It is believed that Mirza Rey Krishna, his grandfather, was the only millionaire in the subcontinent at the time when he built their gigantic mansion. Through his generous encouragement, Mirza Rey Krishna enabled many children's novelists to become famous, who all benefited from his literary pursuits and his generous support.

Haydar's grandfather must have instilled this quality in Hayder because all the stories he has written so far could be published in at least twenty-five books. But instead of being a writer for his own books, he was a sponsor for a number of new writers, paying for them with the money he earned as a writer and not with his inheritance.

I'm very certain that this is not a matter of remuneration that he might have a problem with and has decided to stop writing to us. There is a good chance that he might be ill or have gone somewhere.

There is not a single thing I would not like to boast about him. I had decided that when the chance arose, I would run a full-length interview with him for my magazine at the earliest possibility. I thought I might try persuading him that evening. Though he disliked self-promotion, he surely wouldn't want to disappoint his readers, since they were the very reason he wrote.

Anyway, when I reached Haydar's place, it was almost dusk.

It drizzled.

A few times, like a serpent's tongue, a silent fork of lightning flashed across the sky like a ray of light, only to disappear again into the darkness of the night sky.

The heavy layers of clothing I was wearing and the sturdy shoes I wore didn't make me feel that much warmer, even though I was protected from the rain by my raincoat. Due to my frequent visits to Hayder's house during the launch of our first issue, *The Ghosts*, everyone there knew me quite well. "Everyone" included the caretaker Madris Mia, the chauffeur Abdullah and the cook Hekmat Ali.

Haydar's writing career kept him busy, so he wasn't ready to get married yet. When Hayder's father, Bimal Mirja, passed away almost three years ago, he sent his mother to join his sister in America. He manages the family heritage, his own career alone due to being the only man in the family.

It has been quite some time since I have been here or visited Haydar.

Hekmat Ali is usually the one to open the door in the house, but this time to my utter surprise, it was Hayder himself who walked up to open the door.

Inquiring as to what was wrong, I asked, "Where are you Haydar!" I enquired. "Where is everyone else?"

Hayder smiled at me, as if he could read my thoughts. There was no energy in his voice for even a word to be pronounced, so he just pointed me to step in and did not respond to any of my questions that I had.

Haydar is in such an awful state!

It looked like a skull where his face was supposed to be and his hair was unkempt. His clothes were frayed from neglect and he looked as though he hadn't taken a shower for a very long time. His eye sockets were larger than his eyes. In no way did the man I was looking at resemble the strong, very tall and healthy Hayder Krishna I knew.

"Don't look so surprised, Hasan. Come on in," said Hayder, in a choked-up voice. He looked as if he had aged a few decades since I had last seen him.

I walked into the living room and turned around.

Shutting the door, Haydar stood facing me.

His dryness causes the tallness of his body to bend slightly more.

I couldn't bear the sight of him in this state. Totally dumbfounded, I had no words to describe my feelings.

I sat down at his request. Also, he is facing me when he sits down.11

"What's the matter?" I asked. This is how we cut to the chase. Generally, we don't bother with formalities.

"Nothing special," replied Hayder. "I've dismissed the staff."

My shock was even greater when I heard that. "How do you manage your daily chores then?"

"I managed," he replied with frightening indifference.

"Hayder, tell me the truth. What is going on?"

"I swear, nothing serious," he muttered, as if speaking to himself.

"I don't believe you!" I practically shouted as my patience wore out. "You have to tell me the truth!"

But looking at his face, it was obvious that he had objected to my interrogation. Due to this, I grudgingly stopped asking him questions. As if remembering something, Hayder stood up and asked me to wait in his study room while he made tea for us both. I realised that, due to the heat of the conversation, I had forgotten about the cold weather and that tea was a good idea. While stuck in traffic, I finished mine long before.

Are you sure you can? I wanted to ask, wanting to help him, but before I could even finish my question, he had bolted towards the kitchen.

I went to his study.

Everything was the same as it always had been, though a bit untidy perhaps.

I was just beginning to reminisce about my last visit when I noticed a door on the floor that I couldn't remember seeing before.

Where did that come from? I wondered.

As I approached the door out of sheer curiosity, I felt a chill run down my spine. And at that very moment there was a deafening clap of thunder somewhere very close by.

I was startled and all of a sudden very scared.

It was as if something inside me was warning me with an unholy omen and my heart screamed out, *R-U-N!*

But I managed to control myself and, dismissing such stupid ideas, I opened the door without a second thought.

There is a staircase going straight down somewhere in the building. Rather than waiting for Haydar, I decided to go down.

The room was filled with five coffins that were arranged in a row along the wall!

How on earth did these coffins get here? I asked myself.

The room seemed like a basement and was

damp, dark and dingy. It seemed to me that it was a kind of utility room in the basement.

I noticed, in the corner of the ceiling, there is a ventilator that brings some natural light in from the outside, making this room a little visible without any lights on.

I checked for switches to see if there are any lights.

It wasn't where it should have been.

Slowly, I felt an uncanny fear rising inside me.

I could hardly believe what I was seeing.

But again, I managed to calm myself.

My curiosity led me to open the first coffin.

It was as if I was hypnotised by fear that I opened all three coffins except for the last one, but because it was so dark, I couldn't see clearly what was inside them. And then, as if to fulfil my wish, a flash of lightning lit up the whole basement like daylight.

For a split second, I was able to see what was in the coffins and an icy wave of fright froze me where I stood. My mouth opened wide from the shock and terror of what I had just witnessed!

It was an ear-splitting scream that brought me back to my sense.

My eyes grew wide when I looked over and saw Hayder standing at the door above the staircase, casting an enormous shadow on it as he moved.

It seems that my breath froze inside my chest when I saw what he was devouring, and I felt like my heart would stop!

There was a hand that had been torn from the corpse of a human.

The way Haydar held it, it looked as if he was eating it!

"I have been waiting for someone to come, and now I am hungry." Haydar is no longer Haydar; in fact, it is a Jinn in form of Haydar, who loves eating animal bones, but he has now adapted to eating human bones, apparently!

"There were no bones left! I'm glad you came." The eyes of the creature looked like they had been engulfed in fire.

In that moment, I felt like I was going to lose my mind.

I looked at the coffins one last time.

Right next to the corpses of Hekmat Ali, Madris Mia and Abdullah was another one.

Silent, still and rotten, with blood clots on its torn skin. Just like the other corpses.

It was Haydar's corpse lying on coffin number four!

Looking back at Hayder, my heart almost burst.

He stood inches away now.

I could see him clearly.

It was as if he had just come straight from the pit of hell, because the smell of his breath was so strong.

In my mind, I recited Ayatul Kurshi, the Throne Verse, which is the 255th verse in Chapter two of the Quran. According to the verse, nothing and no one is considered to be comparable to Allah in the eyes of the believers.

Reciting this verse is often very effective in warding off any Jinn that may be present. Then, my final words that I was able to say out loud as I was not surprised that today was my last…

"*Lā ʾIlāha ʾIllā Llāhu Muḥammadur Rasūlu Llāh, There is no deity but God; Muhammad (peace be upon him) is the messenger of God.*"

Just before losing my senses, I heard thunder strike one last time, shaking heaven and earth, as if mocking my fate. It seemed to be saying, *There's going to be another coffin, coffin number five! There's going to be another body, with Hayder Krishna and the rest….* And guess who that is?

———

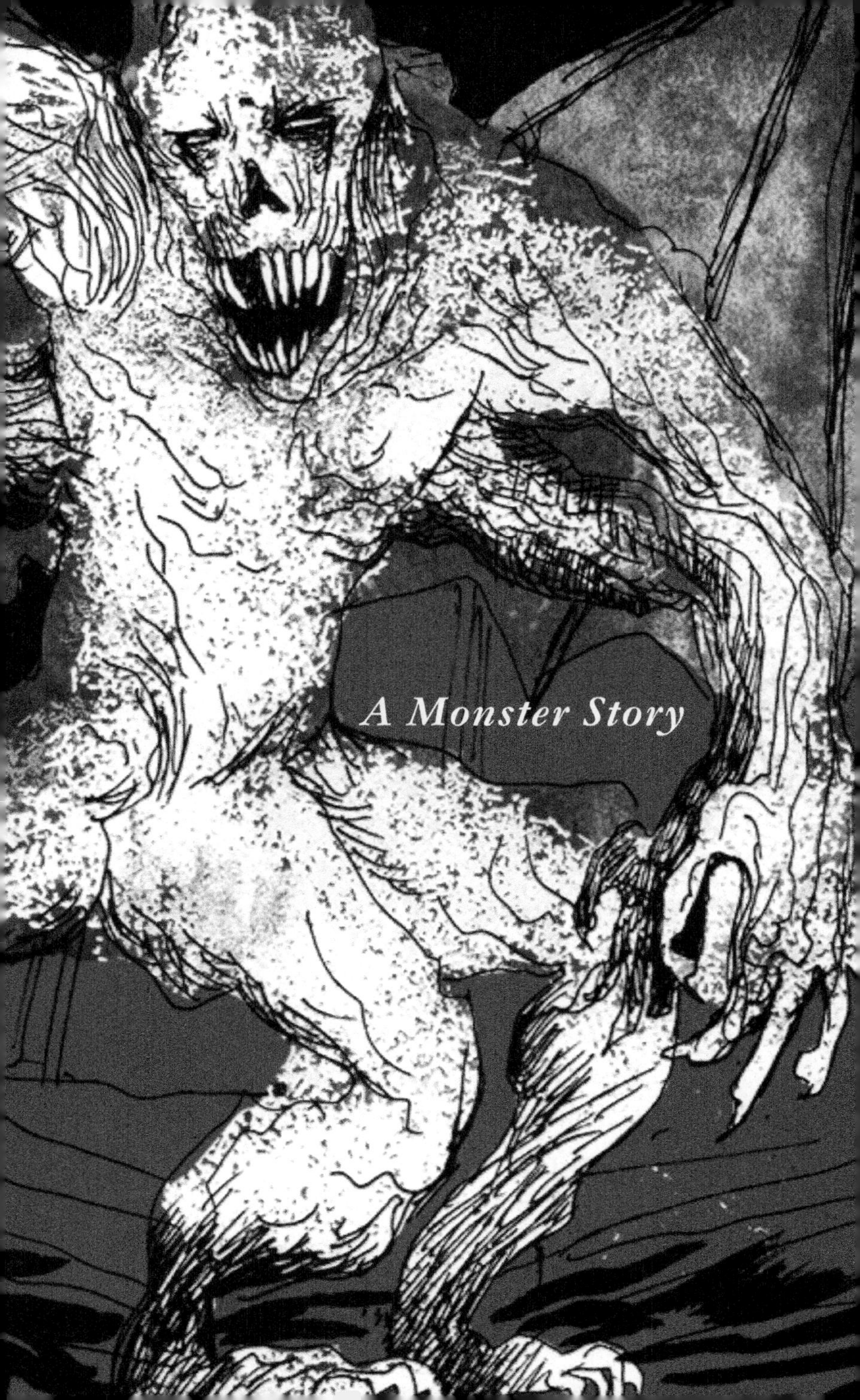
A Monster Story

THE ILLUSION

A lone structure at the top of the hill cast an ominous shadow.

It was a huge building, which had probably once been home to the local overlord, but was now an abandoned ruin. The plaster on the walls was peeling off in places and parts of the walls themselves were crumbling.

It was obvious that no-one lived there any more.

Allen, aged around 14, was standing on an isolated hill path, scrutinising the edifice at the top with a pair of binoculars.

She had arrived a week before with her family to visit Srimangal in the mountainous region near Sylhet. They were staying in a cottage in the city. They were from the Mirpur, capital Dhaka and Allen had never seen tea plantations or such hilly relief before, which was why she had asked her father to take her to a place with hills, forests and tea gardens during the summer vacation. Her father could not refuse such a request from his only daughter. He felt it was a shame that she had already grown up and yet never seen Sylhet, so he had agreed to take the whole family there for a holiday.

On arrival in Sylhet, Allen was charmed by the natural beauty of the city and felt really happy to be there. A huge difference exists between Dhaka and Sylhet. One of the best things about the place was the weather, which was so much better than in Dhaka. There was such an air of purity about everything, a true sense of natural beauty!

Allen drew in a long breath and took the binoculars from her eyes. The day was warm, with a soft breeze which ruffled her hair.

She was much intrigued by the massive building at the top of the hill and wanted to go and explore it, but she could not find a path that led up to it. She made several attempts to climb up the slope but was prevented from getting very far by the thick bushes and debris all around. But she was determined that she would get there at all costs, even though it was almost lunch time and she had left the cottage early in the morning. She had been wandering around all morning and had somehow ended up in this hilly area.

After spotting the building, she had spent the past few hours trying to reach it. But without success.

After scouring the hillside for a while, Allen finally found a track that seemed to lead to the top of the hill and to the building, although it was impossible to realise that it led up there without looking very closely. The foresters often modified the landscape for the tea plantations, so maybe it was they who had made this path to get up and down the hill.

Allen was feeling very happy and carefree as she started to climb the hill. The higher she got, the wider her view became. The whole city stretched out beneath her and when she reached the summit, she felt that she had achieved something great. She shouted out with joy, her voice echoing all around the tea valley.

She could see the buildings of the city far away and imagined the noise and bustle going on there, while here, surrounded by nature, there was an odd sort of silence.

Now Allen concentrated on the building.

There was no sign of life. The place was covered with trees and bushes.

It had just one entrance and she made her way towards it. She crossed the lawn to the terrace, looking all around her with curiosity.

The building was full of moss and weeds. The walls were cracked and the bricks and stones were falling apart. The windows and ceilings were completely covered in cobwebs. The terrace was quite small, with an abandoned well on its right. The well had no water in it but was full of dead branches.

Allen turned left to visit the rooms on the ground

floor.

She thoroughly examined each and every room. Although there was no longer anything special, it was apparent that the place had once been quite luxurious.

After checking the rooms on the left, Allen walked towards the doorway that led to the only room on the right side of the building.

The door itself was lying on the floor, broken and almost completely eaten up by beetles.

She went into the room, where the midday sunlight was filtering through the windows, making it quite bright.

The room was fairly big and had perhaps once been the living room. Everything was covered in dust.

There was no furniture left. It had probably all been stolen a long time ago. It appears that all the wooden items, such as windows, doors, shutters, and staircases, are gone like they were savagely eaten by rare insects.

Allen had found what she was looking for - the stairs to the second floor. She was surprised that it had taken her so long to find it. Although the staircase is badly eaten, it is still possible to go up.

Allen ran upstairs, with a feeling of excited expectation. She looked out at the mountains, standing like sentinels in the distance. Somewhere close by a flock of sparrows started chirping.

She explored all the rooms on the second floor. There was a kitchen, drawing room, study, guest room, all containing old, dilapidated furniture. Bitten and eaten!

Allen went into one of the rooms and suddenly froze in her tracks! There was a statue standing in the corner, but not of a human form. It was a statue of the kind of beast that only exists in mythical stories or movies, an unearthly creature.

The statue had four hands, wings like a bat and three legs arranged like a tripod. Its face looked like a wolf's. But there was something else as well.

There was blood!

Fresh blood was dripping from the beast's mouth! This creature appears to eat everything wood, causing injuries to its teeth and gums.

Allen was terrified. What on earth could it mean?

She suddenly got the impression that the statue was alive. The beast's mouth was moving slightly and its whole body seemed to be quivering.

Allen had never been so scared in all her life. Her heart was beating fit to burst and her mouth had gone completely dry.

At first she thought it was a dream or some sort

of hallucination. But how could she ignore what was clearly happening before her very eyes?

When she looked into the beast's eyes, she became even more terrified. It was now looking straight at her. Her entire body started to shake and she became aware that both her body and her mind were gradually being paralysed as if the beast were hypnotising her!

She suddenly came back to her senses and realised that if she wanted to come out of this experience alive, she had to escape. But as she turned back to run to the door, she found that there was no longer any way out!

Scared to death, Allen looked back at the beast.

It was advancing towards her now.

It was no longer a statue made of stone, but a living creature.

Its body was shining with grease and it was making an ungodly and fearsome noise.

A long serpent-like tongue was dangling from its mouth.

Allen decided that she had to stay alive, no matter what. She looked around the room again, only to find that the room too had disappeared and that she was just surrounded by smoke. She knew that she was trapped.

She looked at the beast. It was advancing very slowly towards her. It's cold, unblinking eyes were fixed on Allen, all ready to pounce on her…

A bit of pain started to be felt on one of her fingers, and she noticed that the finger was turning bone!

#

"Hey there, girl!"

Allen turned round abruptly as she heard a man calling behind her. At first she could not see anything; everything seemed blurred.

The beast standing in front of her had vanished! Gradually, her vision began to clear up. As if she had just returned to reality, everything seemed quiet and normal again.

"What are you doing here?" the man asked from the door. He had unkempt hair and was wearing a guard's uniform. As he held the bamboo stick, he was yelling. "O my God! Where are your parents? Do you not know at such an hour, these places are no good for anyone? No one comes out at such an hour, are you for real?"

"Um… I was just wandering around a bit. Who

are you?" Allen said.

"Who I am is none of your business. Didn't you know it's not safe to wander around this place? Especially alone! There is a warning board down there, didn't you noticed it?" the man replied, waving his bamboo stick at her.

"I wonder why there is no one outside in such a beautiful midday?"

"In the middle of the day, the tea gardens are unsuitable for visits. Better hurry!"

"You're right... I realised that from what just happened a moment ago!" said Allen as she started to leave the room.

"What do you mean?" the man asked from behind.

But Allen had taken to her heels. She had to get out of that cursed building as soon as she could. It was two by two that she descended the stairs and beat a hasty retreat from the house.

Suddenly remembering the man, she turned round. On the front lawn of the house, she stood in the middle of the grass.

She noticed for the first time that there were many broken bird bones scattered around the area and it was a very disturbing sight.

But the man was nowhere to be seen! Was it all just a hoax? No, how could that be possible?

The man had talked to her. How could he just vanish? Did he stay upstairs?

Suddenly the whole place started shaking before her eyes, as if it were floating in the air. What was going on? Everything was vanishing right before her eyes!

There has long been a conjecture about what can happen in Sylhet's hilly zone at noon.

There used to be a saying that if you went out alone to a tea garden hills at midday you would run the risk of being possessed by evil spirits. If they could have the power to enchant you, they would be able to make you disappear forever!

Allen fell to the ground, helpless and senseless. It didn't matter how it happened, she ended up in a demon's lair. Little did she know what a great peril she had just escaped from!

Beware of this warning and heed it - Never, under any circumstances, go anywhere alone during the midday hour. And especially if you ever get the chance to visit the tea mountains of Sylhet.

They eat bones!

A Haunting Story

THE DARK KEEPER

It is not unusual for a midnight horror story to take place in a haunted house or even in a deep tunnel as either of these locations are often depicted as the setting of the story. It seems that in order to make the story uncanny, central focus would have to be a century-old abandoned building.

But, Mr. Siddique's guest house appeared to be nothing like that, despite the fact that it had been empty for years.

Well, the building was certainly not entirely empty since there was a caretaker- Ganesh Chatterjee, around a 60 year-old man, who has been maintaining the place for quite some time now.

Since Mr. Siddique was living with his family abroad, he has hardly come over and stayed here. Having stayed here with his family a month earlier, Mr. Siddique was not certain if he would have the opportunity to return here in the near future. Usually, he returns every other year, along with his family, just to check up on his inheritance and to make sure everything is in order.

The family had employed Ganesh Chatterjee for a long time. It was because he was a really trustworthy person that Mr. Siddique was quite confident to entrust Ganesh with the responsibility of maintaining this house to him.

The main focus of the story may seem to be the house of Mr. Siddique, yes, that's partially true, but aside from the house being the part of the story that primarily served as a backdrop to the story, it wasn't the main focal point throughout the entire piece. Let's get to it.

It was a Monday afternoon, around 2 P.M.

It was just now that Ganesh realised that he had left his shawl in the grocery store. Considering it was winter time, he always wore a big shawl around himself when he go out, so as to keep himself warm while he walked. He was rather cross with himself. But he did not feel like going back there just to fetch the shawl. He will be doing some grocery shopping the following day anyway, so he will retrieve it when he does that. He knew the shopkeeper so he was sure he wouldn't lose his shawl.

Ganesh made two cups of tea and went out onto the terrace.

He was feeling relaxed. Then he noticed that Muhin was stroking his dog.

Ganesh's pet black dog seemed very happy to receive such affection from Muhin. As Ganesh saw Muhin's backpack next to the wooden chair, it took him a few moments to realise that it was full of clothes, which would only mean that the Muhin would be staying there for a while.

This guy had caught Ganesh's attention as he was returning from the shop. He looked for Mr. Siddique's guest house. It was then that he asked who the man was and he replied that he was a friend of Mr. Siddique's. His name was Muhin Khan.

It was indeed true that Mr. Siddique had informed Ganesh that a friend of his would be staying with him for a few days at the guest house. He had asked Ganesh to take good care of Muhin. In fact, Ganesh felt quite delighted to have a guest in this house. At least there would be someone to talk to!

It is common for Ganesh to spend most of his time talking to his dog, as there is no other option for him. There is just no way he could go to the hut every day for the sake of talking, and there are not many people around.

Muhin seemed quite healthy for a person of his age, since he had the same age as Mr. Siddique, but Mr. Siddique was quite the opposite of Muhin.

Ganesh had no idea why Muhin had come but that was not a problem. There would be plenty of time for him to ask.

“Have a cup of tea. I just made it,” said Ganesh, handing a cup to Muhin.

Muhin was kneeling next to the dog. In response, he stood up and went to sit on the wooden chair and accepted the cup.

“You have such a cute dog. I like him very much. What’s his name?” asked Muhin as he sipped his cup of tea.

“He acts like a sherr, a tiger, which is why I call him Sherr. But he’s not as gentle as you would think.” Ganesh replied.

“Really?”

“Yes, I guard this house and Sherr guards me.”

“Wow! That’s interesting!”

“Well, yes. But I can see he likes you and now he’s going to bug you all the time.”

“Don’t worry about that. I love animals. In fact, I would actually quite like that.”

“Good for you then.”

Teatime was spent with small talk like this. Then

Ganesh prepared the room where Muhin would be staying.

That night at dinner, Muhin pretty much forced Ganesh to sit with him at the table to eat together.

#

The next day.

Muhin spent almost the entire day exploring the area. Ganesh wasn't in the house when he returned. There was no one in the house except for him. He assumed that Sherr had been out with Ganesh as well.

Muhin began to survey the house as he looked around.

Although it was only a single-story building, it was huge in terms of size. It had at least fifteen rooms. There were two rooms next to the staircase that led up to the roof.

They were locked.

Looking at the locks, it was obvious that no one had entered those rooms for a long while. There were cobwebs all over the door handles.

There was no doubt in Muhin's mind that these

were the rooms that Mr. Siddique never used when he was here to stay. He started thinking about what could be inside those rooms out of the blue!

Mr. Siddique seems like he is a pretty wealthy guy; Muhin is inclined to think that the house he is staying in must be crammed full of valuable possessions. It is possible for even the most mundane places to hide gold mines!

The relationship between Muhin and Mr. Siddique was that of a friendly acquaintance, but they weren't really close friends. A long time ago, Mr. Siddique had been to visit Cox's Bazaar as tourist with his family. He had met Muhin at a restaurant that he-frequented there. Muhin was a member of one of the tourist clubs. His job was to provide the tourists with guides. That was when they had become known to each other. Mr. Siddique gave Muhin his address and said that if he ever needed to, he could move to this house. That was how Muhin had come to be there now, after checking with Mr. Siddique.

He found the place quite pleasant.

It was surrounded by a tea garden all around and

was far from the hustle and bustle of the city, so it was very relaxing. It was a great choice for Mr. Siddique to put this guest house in this location.

Muhin was very pleased.

He was quite sure that the next few days would be great for him.

#

Ganesh rushed back to the guest house. He was walking very fast.

There was already dusk on the horizon. Ganesh was carrying two bags full of groceries, as well as the shawl he had retrieved from the shop.

There seemed to be something bugging him as he looked very agitated. He was shaking his head every once in a while, thinking of something.

Sherr was leading the way.

A couple of men had approached Ganesh at the grocery store to talk to him. They had drawn him aside to a quiet corner of the shop and told him something that he was still finding hard to believe.

They said they were detectives and that they were from the police department.

At first, Ganesh thought that they were lying to

him, but once they showed him some newspaper clippings from a number of newspapers, he realised that they were telling the truth.

It was all about Muhin Khan in the news, along with a photo of him!

Apparently, Muhin Khan had murdered some tourists a week before and had fled with over half a million! He was wanted by the police and they were trying to catch him.

The police had followed Muhin to the guest house, but were unable to arrest him until they had taken down the rest of the criminals associated with the murders. They wanted to arrest them all at the same time for the sake of maintaining order. The case is extremely sensitive, and the moment they catch Muhin with the rest of the evidence, they will definitely hang him to death.

Having asked Ganesh for help, the detectives hoped Ganesh would be able to help them.

Sherr had sensed the tension as well.

Ganesh was afraid that Muhin would also perceive it and may try to do something wrong…

Ganesh hastened his steps.

#

As the entire building was dark, the only light coming from the lamppost on the front lawn was enough to illuminate some of the interior, but this was so deemed that the darkness could not be any lesser.

Muhin had just received a call from someone.

He was informed by his boss that the police had discovered the location of where he was staying. He had to get away as soon as possible.

In order to get his bag packed as quickly as possible before Ganesh got back, Muhin was frantically packing it.

There was a long period of time that Muhin was faded up with his guide job. As a result of doing the job honestly, he did not receive a good salary, nor did he receive any respect for it. It just does not make sense to him why employers do not want to respect the people who work hard and try to make a living from their only occupation. He used to be forced to work overtime without receiving any compensation or bonus. He was unable to do any other job to cover his expenses. It was a rule that he had to return all tips he received to his employer, no matter how much they were! There used to be a little percentage that he used to get from all the tips he received. Muhin was having the worst nightmare of his life. It was a situation that he wanted to escape from at all costs. He then met Mr. Qubrik, a powerful gang leader who kills rich tourists for money. He actually pays others to do the killing for him, instead of doing it all himself.

Last week, it was Tuesday.

He was dropping off his tourists at individual hotels, Mr. Qubrik, and his target group was the last group of people in the jeep that he was dropping off at the hotels. Apart from Muhin and Mr. Qubrik, they were a total of three people.

Qubrik offered Muhin something that he would not be able to earn even if he worked five years in a row as a guide! That night he was already exhausted, irritated, and frazzled. In such a state, he just couldn't resist the offer to help Qubrik shoot those tourists!

They left the dead bodies. Then Qubrik gave him some cash, still a jaw dropping amount, and told him to hide somewhere…

First time in Muhin's life, he saw a massive amount of money! The only thing he was truly obsessive about was having a huge amount of money by doing such an *easy* job! The feeling of hunger he felt at that moment had just begun to overwhelm him...

Muhin broke the locks on the two rooms next to the staircase. What he found there was beyond his expectations.

He found carats of pure gold jewellery and some silverware! There was no doubt in his mind that by selling those things, he would be able to make quite a bit of more money.

It did not take him long to pack them into another bag as well.

The moment he finished packing, he made his way to the door, but as he stepped out, he was surprised to see Ganesh standing there waiting for him!

"It really doesn't matter what you did before you came here." Ganesh tells Muhin in a cold tone, trying to get him to pay attention to him. "But I do care about what you're doing right now. You shouldn't do that. I suggest you leave the things that you're trying to take away from here."

"Oh, stay away, you old man!" Muhin, desperate to escape, had pushed Ganesh away and run towards the exit.

Ganesh had fallen to the ground, but managed to get up again to run outside after hearing a frightening scream as if someone was dying.

There was something very unusual going on outside!

Sherr!

He had turned into a monster!

Muhin had been dragged from one side of the yard to the other by a normal-sized dog, Sherr, possessed of an ungodly amount of strength, tearing him limb from limb!

That is what Ganesh had meant when he had told Muhin earlier on that Sherr was not as gentle as he might think. Clearly, Muhin didn't understand what he was saying.

This was nothing new to Ganesh though.

There was a strange news circulating a few

months ago that Ramij the robber had gone missing, and it was a bit strange news. It was unknown what happened to Ramij. He actually had come to rob this guest house. Somehow, they guessed that this house held something valuable. But Ganesh was ready to die if it was necessary to save everything in the house, and his pet Sherr was determined to save his master's life if he had to.

Ganesh wanted Ramji to know Sherr isn't just any dog, it's taken care of by a dark Jinn only listening to Ganesh!

The fate of Ramij the robber was sealed on that stormy night when he met his demise. Sherr had killed him without mercy! But that's another story.

This will be the end of the story of Muhin, as tonight will once again be the night when Muhin will face the same fate as Ramji!

Devastated Muhin was horrified to see a bone eater, uncanny figure approaching him step by step.

A Psychopath Horror

THE EGYPTIAN SKELETON

There were only two living people and one lifeless object sitting in the train compartment.

It might seem odd that to describe a lifeless object as "sitting", but the reason for describing it that way is quite logical in the end. Since the object used to have life in it, but as the life was no longer there, it was more appropriate to refer to it as lifeless, and at the same time it was also appropriate to refer to it as sitting in a compartment, as the object was a skeleton of a person that had died not long ago!

The skeleton belongs to Mr. Moinuddin. He was one of the two people who were sitting in the compartment next to the skeleton. Roich Uddin, a doctor, who sat opposite Moinuddin. The doctor was focused exclusively on the skeleton. Moinuddin had the skeleton sitting up like a living human being.

The doctor had no doubts about where the skeleton came from. Moinuddin had told him that he had collected the skeleton from Egypt during the many years he spent in that country. The skeleton was found when he was excavating some old graves with an archaeologist who later gave the skeleton to him as a gift!

There was no way the doctor could interpret that, for who in their right mind would give a skeleton as a gift to a man, after all? As a simple matter of fact, it was quite easy to assume that Moinuddin was insane. Otherwise, why would an old man move around with a skeleton on his back?

In order to give Moinuddin some treatment at home without his knowledge, Roich Uddin planned to take the patient home with him. To deal with Moinuddin's strange attitude, his wife, who happened to be Roich Uddin's younger sister, had asked him to take a look at the situation since she was fed up with Moinuddin's strange behaviour.

So, doctor Roich Uddin took Moinuddin to his home under the pretext that they had an invitation from his family. The skeleton was bothering him a lot.

Dr. Roich is a little shivered when he sees the uncanny appearance of it. There was nothing he hated more than skeletons.

During his time as a student at a medical college, some of his classmates had pulled a prank on him with a skeleton! If there had been some other people in the compartment he wouldn't have cared less about skeletons, but it was quite difficult to be in the same compartment with a skeleton and a mentally imbalanced person.

Dr. Roich had a great urge to throw the skeleton out of the window, but he was unsure about Moinuddin's reaction. Because he didn't know what to do, he went and sat down next to the skeleton. But one could tell by his inertia and discomfort that he did not like this lifeless skeleton at all.

Little did he know how great a price he would have to pay!

#

It would be wrong to assume that Mr. Moinuddin was ignoring the speed of the train and just enjoying the view. Although he seemed bright and cheery, his attention was in fact completely on his brother-in-law, Roich Uddin.

Why was he looking at the skeleton like that?

What was his intention?

Was he trying to steal his favourite skeleton?

Well, maybe that was what he was planning. Otherwise why would he invite him all of a sudden? A person who had never even had much respect for him, why would he force Moinuddin to go to his house now?

No! He must have had bad intentions!

If he hadn't been his wife's older brother, Moinuddin would already have asked him directly what his intentions were. But he changed the subject and said to Roich Uddin, "Come and sit next to me, Brother."

This rather abrupt invitation brought Roich

Uddin back to reality. Up to then he had been observing the skeleton.

Although he couldn't understand why Moinuddin asked him to sit next to him, he complied without saying anything. However, when he glanced at Moinuddin, he saw that the latter was looking very angry. His face was red and his eyes were burning. For all his life Roich Uddin couldn't understand the reason for Moinuddin's sudden anger, but he was afraid. He also realised that something terrible, uncanny was about to happen. And before he could finish his thoughts…

#

"You know what, Rehnuma? I will tell anyone about the skeleton that it is a gift. No one knows that it's that archaeologist's skeleton! I can't believe that man wanted to kill me!" Moinuddin burst out laughing as he dropped the pair of skeletons on the bed. His wife, Rehnuma, struck her forehead desperately with her hands. As if one skeleton wasn't enough! Now there are two! In a frustrated voice she asked, "Is it also from Egypt?"

"No, it's freshly made here."

"It looks like someone else tried to kill you!"

Moinuddin previously told her he was concerned

about the archaeologist working with him. The man kept telling him he should see a doctor, and sometimes he even called him crazy! Moinuddin knows sometimes he doesn't make sense, but that doesn't mean people should call him crazy. He doesn't understand why people are jealous of his success!

"Yes, your brother, Roich Uddin." Moinuddin paused. He knew Rehnuma Begum would probably have a nervous breakdown now and lose her senses. That wasn't really a problem though. He would just call a doctor.

He gazed unperturbedly at his wife and said, "You know very well, I don't like tricks." There was a mysterious smile on Moinuddin's lips. It wasn't like the smile of a drunk or an insane person.

It was the smile of a sick psychopath. With the babble of a senseless man, Moinuddin said one last thing, "But if someone asks, tell them this one is from Egypt too."

Mrs. Rehnuma understood that if she ever gave her husband the impression that she was indifferent to his skeletal state, or even doubting him for it, she might end up being the next Egyptian skeleton he had to carry!

———

An Occult Horror

THE MUSEUM OF HEIGHTS

It was not long after Mr. Romanath Chakraborty entered his office that his secretary Sudhanath Bardhan dashed towards him.

There was something amusing about the way Sudhanath was rushing along that made Romanath suppress a rising urge to laugh. Then he handed Sudhanath his briefcase and arranged his tie.

"What's up, Shubodh?" he asked Sudhanath. "Anything special?" He usually called Sudhanath by the name Shubodh as it was much easier to pronounce.

"Yes, sir. The people who were supposed to come from the press…"

"Did they call to confirm?" Romanath interrupted him.

Shubodh was silent. He looked down at his black and white uniform for a second.

"Well, they called but…" Shubodh replied in a tense voice.

"So they aren't coming, right?" Romanath seemed relieved. "I myself asked them not to come but I thought they would anyway. Are you familiar with the way news reporters work? It's better if they don't show up."

The smile returned to Shubodh's face as he continued, "Oh, that's awesome, sir…" It was his fear that Romanath would be furious if he found out he couldn't handle the journalists and he would be mad at him for it.

Romanath picked up one of the old newspapers that were piled on the desk. He then pointed out to Shubodh the news that was highlighted, reading it aloud: "*THE MONA LISA SCULPTURE HAS BEEN GIVEN TO THE MEUSUM OF HEIGHTS*... you see! I tried to hide this so hard, but these press people got the news and spread it! Now, I am inviting them to come and feature us as part of Prof. Saiman Chowdhury's dad's sculpture...hmm, no one seems to have said a word!" Grumbling, he threw the newspaper back into the pile.

"Oh Sir, the professor called me a while ago!" Shubodh shoot it quickly as he suddenly remembered. Having made a mistake already, he don't want to make one again.

Romanath had just set up his desk and was reclining in his chair, he almost jumped out of his chair.

"What! He should have been here by now, then!" He exclaimed.

"Yes, sir, he said he'd be here soon."

As Romanath rummaged through his wallet, he pulled out some banknotes. He handed them to Shubodh. "Make us some nice cup of tea and ask Vikram to open the museum's doors. Go, fast!"

Shubodh took the money and left.

Romanath looked at his wristwatch. It was ten minutes past nine. Taking a moment to dial a number, he hurriedly pushed the wrong number. Then he tried it again and it worked this time.

"Good morning, Ranjeet? Yes, the professor is on his way," Romanath informed the person on the other end. "...If that is the case, I will put it in the refrigerator for the time being... I'll speak to my superiors about setting up an exhibition.... It would be great if you could attend. But never mind if you can't... Talk to you later, bye." As Romanath put down the phone, he could hear a car stopping outside.

It was probably Professor Saiman Chowdhury.

A smile radiated across Romanath Chakraborty's face. He looked exceptionally happy as he walked towards the door to receive the professor, arranging his suit and tie as he did so.

#

Professor Saiman Chowdhury looked at the sculpture inside the glass box for the very last time.

It had been almost seven years since someone had made the sculpture. It was a wonderful effigy of his late father.

Professor Saiman had donated it to this museum in the hopes that they will preserve it in the best possible way for the future.

He was quite aged himself. Sixty to be precise. Having already suffered two heart attacks, it is not a stretch of the imagination to say that his health wasn't so great either.

Professor had not exactly earned a lot in his lifetime, owning only a few acres of land and a large house, but he was very proud of the accomplishments he had been able to achieve and of the fact that he worked as a professor as well. He was quite content with the way his life had turned out, as he had succeeded in fulfilling all his desires to the best of his ability. He believed that he was perhaps the only person who had the ability to call himself truly happy.

A benign modesty filled Romanath's tone as he assured the professor, "Sir, we promise to exhibit your sculpture in the proper manner."

"Thank you very much, Mr. Romanath. There is no doubt in my mind that you will. I would like you to remember that I am making this wish as my last wish." Professor said.

"Rest assured, sir. From today on it will be an asset to the museum." he promised the professor. "And I'm sure you realise how important such assets are to us."

"Well, that's good to hear." Professor said gratefully. Then he passed the cup of tea that he had just finished to Romanath. Romanath was already holding his finished cup, but he wasn't bothered by holding both empty cups at once, since he was so excited about the new sculpture.

Basically, what he wants is for the Professor to leave.

Romanath accompanied the professor to his car and helped him get into it.

When he returned to his office, he asked Shubodh to bring him another hot cup of tea. Shubodh immediately went to make another fresh cup of tea for Romanath. He just does not like tea at all! It is not a problem for him to make tea for Romanath, though. He spent the last three years working with Romanath at this job, and he realised that he only asks for tea when he has something specific in mind!

#

At around noon, Romanath Chakraborty rushed back home.

His wife, Lata Chakraborty, was chatting to the

woman who lived next door. The woman was called Abida Hasan. Her husband Hasan Rahman was an engineer and she was a housewife.

"What's the matter, Lata? Your husband seems to be in an awful hurry!" Abida joked.

"I think he has to go somewhere. He never has lunch at home," Lata explained.

"Uh oh, I guess this is a bad time then, should I come back later?" asked Abida, looking a bit awkward.

"No, no. Trust me, He'll go out again right away," Lata laughed.

Romanath Chakraborty proved his wife right. He had taken the time just to have a shower and change his clothes. He looked very smart in a white shirt and brown trousers.

"Lata, I'm so sorry, I have to go somewhere now. I'll be back shortly," he said to his wife.

"Where are you going at this time of the day?" Lata asked him.

"I have a few errands to do." Romanath replied evasively and suggested that Abida have lunch with Lata. Then he rushed out without even waiting for Abida to reply.

He took a rickshaw.

He had to get to Ranjeet's place as soon as possible. Ranjeet was the person who had made the sculpture of Professor Saiman Chowdhury's father.

#

"What you're saying is that you can turn this statue into gold, aren't you?" Romanath asked Ranjeet with utter disbelief in his voice.

Ranjeet Malik didn't reply, he was too absorbed in cleaning the statue of Saiman Chowdhury's father.

"Hey, why aren't you answering my question?" asked Romanath impatiently.

When Ranjeet finished brushing off the last bit of dust from the sculpture, he said, "Hold on a minute Romanath!" as he stood back to watch.

It was immediately after Professor Saiman Chowdhury had left the museum that Romanath arranged to have the sculpture sent to Ranjeet for him to examine. They had been close friends for almost twenty years. There was a time when Ranjeet was quite poor and always had trouble paying his bills on time. At the time when Romanath got hired at the museum ten years ago, Ranjeet was searching desperately for a job to support his family.

Ranjeet was a skilled sculptor and was excellent at making exact likenesses of the people he sculpted. However, that was not exactly a stable source of income for him, and the pay for his work was not even very good.

Over the last couple of months, Romanath had noticed that Ranjeet's financial situation has drastically improved. Overnight he had bought a new cars, a large house and a few plots of land, all of which were almost all new to him.

Romanath had asked him a few days ago what was going on in his life. Even though Ranjeet appeared to be evasive at first, he eventually revealed his secret, because Romanath wouldn't let the matter go without a fight.

"I've learned how to turn the sculptures of dead men into gold, my friend!" Ranjeet confided with a crooked smile on his face.

The first thought that passed through Romanath's mind was that this was the greatest nonsense he had heard in his entire life. However, he still asked for proof to prove his claim.

Ranjeet feigned the appearance of indifference as he said, "I don't really have anything to show you right now, but there is something you can do," Then he added- "I sculpted an effigy of Professor Saiman Chowdhury's father Dr. Afzal Chowdhury. If you can get it for me, then I can show you how it's done."

"A long walk just for the sake of getting a cup of tea? That's a TON of nonsense to me! Why don't you make a sculpture of me and turn it into a gold?" From Romanath's tone of voice it was obvious he was mocking his friend.

"I told you it had to be a statue of a dead man. I have the statue of Dr. Afzal Chowdhury; he has now passed away so…"

Romanath couldn't let this go.

He decided he would get the statue and see the end of Ranjeet's nonsense. But the son of Dr. Afzal Chowdhury, Professor Saiman Chowdhury, was quite an influential person in the town, so Romanath was not sure how to get the statue from him.

That's when it occurred to Romanath to use the museum. And it didn't take much; all he did was write an official letter asking professor Saiman if he would allow the museum to preserve the statue of Dr. Afzal. And that worked like magic!

It was now time to watch Ranjeet's trick.

"Let me tell you what happened first," Ranjeet began, speaking in a very pleasant tone. "The last time I went to Rangamati was a few months ago, right? I'm sure you're aware of that. The other day I went out for a walk at a quiet time, and out of nowhere a monk appeared in front of me. I'll never forget that experience! He told me to drink some blood and I could turn the statues I make into gold by using a drop of my own blood. But it had to be a statue of a deceased person."

In the midst of his thoughts, Ranjeet paused. Then he pointed to the portrait of Rabindranath Tagore on the wall and said, "I made a statue of him. Although it was a challenge, I drank the blood of a cow, as the monk had told me."

Romanath felt utterly disgusted at the notion of drinking blood, but he was intrigued nonetheless.

"And then I experimented with the statue," Ranjeet continued. "Whether or not it was successful, you will get to know very soon," he finished, as he picked up a small fruit knife from the table.

Romanath shook in anticipation.

He couldn't believe his own ears.

A monk came to a person and said things that turned out to be true!

But Romanath wanted to see for himself.

Ranjeet placed the index finger of his left hand above the statue. There were some old scars on the finger. From the look of it, the wound was quite deep but had healed. In the direction of the scar, Ranjeet Malik advanced the knife.

He might cut this part again to be able to suck some blood from himself!

#

It happened one morning that there was a shiny Corolla car stopped in front of the MUSEUM OF HEIGHTS. Sudhanath ran to open the car door, but before he could reach it, Romanath stepped out.

"Come on, Shubodh! I've beaten you again!" Romanath said to Sudhanath, with a wide, mocking smile on his face.

Sudhanath had fun laughing at the childish jokes made by his boss.

It was very easy for him to get to the car before Romanath got out, but he did not do that on purpose as he knew that beating "Shubodh" was a form of entertainment for Romanath.

Only a few months ago this man used to come to the office in a rickshaw and now it seems that he had become rich overnight! Sudhanath had never understood how Romanath had made that happen but, frankly, he didn't really care. There is not only a great change in Romanath's wealth, but he has also developed a huge change in his manner as well! The way in which he talks to Shubodh is now very gentle, which is much more important to Shubodh than knowing how this man got so rich.

"Hey Shubodh, bring me a nice cup of tea please!" Romanath requested. As he picked up the newspaper from his desk, he sat back in his chair feeling completely relaxed.

There was an article published in the newspaper that stated as follows:

...The poultry business has become an unimaginably lucrative industry in recent years, and many people are taking advantage of that fact to start new businesses in this sector. Statistics say that the main consumers of poultry are people from the middle and lower classes. Many are selling dozens of chickens as hawkers...

Romanath called Ranjeet before finishing the news.

"We must find another way to collect blood, my friend! If we keep collecting blood from chickens and then sending them back to the market for sale, it might raise suspicion...," Romanath said with something like fear in his voice.

"I've seen the news too," Ranjeet replied on the other side, echoing Romanath's tense voice. "How about making an agreement with a butcher?"

In a matter of a few minutes, the two friends had a solution to their problem, even before Sudhanath had brought Romanath the "nice cup of tea" that he had requested!

#

Mrs. Lata Chakraborty had noticed that ever since her husband had become rich, he had started drinking a lot of red grape juices and she was afraid he might be turning into an alcoholic. The drinks looked exactly like blood. By now she had got used to his drinking habit however and now and then her husband would suggest mockingly, "Would you like to try some?"

———

A Ghost Story

WHEN SHE RETURNED

Keokradong has been the scene of two murders within the past two days.

The villagers were traumatised, even though the people who were killed were not such good people. But they were Idris Molla's closest associates.

Good people like Idris Molla exist.

The village knows him as a respectable person. He is pious and religious, a very kind man. Financially, he is well off, and he helps the needy. By employing two of those bones of the pelvis men, Idris Molla won the hearts of the indigenous villagers. He told the villagers to give these two a chance to prove themselves. The idea occurred to Idris Molla that they might need a stable job and hoped it will change their lives for the better.

Villagers agreed to Idris Molla's decision and were happy to see the two get jobs with Idris Molla. But both of them proved themselves to be the worst in the village and kept bothering everyone!

Idris Molla never poked his nose into other people's business – in fact he couldn't abide by that sort of behaviour. It's been said that he is quite impulsive and is a generous giver, no one has ever complained about him. However, the two men he had employed had used his simplicity and generosity to take advantage of him. They were supposed to look after his tourists who come here for hiking, visiting Keokradong peak, and staying at one of his cottage, but they were more interested in causing trouble in the village than doing their jobs. It took Idris Molla a long time to realise this.

Teasing foreign tourists was an everyday thing for them, but before the villagers had got completely fed up with them and were ready to make complaints against them to Idris Molla, they died.

Some people believed they had been killed by some hot-headed tourists who might had grown frustrated with them.

Idris Molla wanted to file a case with the police, but when he got to know the real truth about his employees, he changed his mind. He asked everyone not to bother about it.

They had been punished for their bad deeds.

Everyone agreed.

Then, four days later, a third murder took place!

#

Professor David Craft, a lecturer from the London School of Economics, came to Sungsawng Para with Muhammed Habibul Islam, a colleague with whom he works in London.

Habibul and he spent a few days in the city last week, and he only learned of the murders when they returned to Sungsawng Para. The fact that no one had contacted the police shocked Mr. David more than the fact that there had been two deaths!

Habibul was born and raised in Sungsawng Para. He used to work as a guide here before he got the chance to move to London. Since he worked as a tourist guide while continuing his studies, he caught villagers' attention and was encouraged to take higher study in London and do something for the community. Having been away from his motherland for almost seven years, Habibul is visiting his own village for the first time now. He did not forget that he had a duty to the community he belongs to.

He has a powerful glass on his eyes that gives him a unique personality. He used to be an unhealthy boy with messy frizzy hair; now he has a fit body and he looks a lot better, much sorted. It is always obvious that poverty has a negative impact on the appearance of humans.

When Habibul was a young man, his dream was to get higher education, get a stable job, and change the lives of others as well. He believes in knowledge. In his return, he only hoped to improve his village through education and employment opportunities.

David Craft had a white beard and a chockfull of a moustache. His shoulder-length hair was as white as snow. His glasses gave away that he might very well be a professor, and it was easy to assume just by looking at him. He didn't look like this seven years ago, when he first met Habibul in London, looking for a room to share. Since then, they have become best friends and colleagues. London is a city that Mr. David loves as he comes from Scotland. He has never been poor, but he has no concept of what it is like not to have access to education, a decent job, or living standards. Habibul taught him about Bangladesh's educational situation during his stay in London, as well as every issue that's been going on in Bangladesh. Considering that Habibul Islam was a great lecturer and is now working in a well-paying position, they both agreed that only education would be able to bring about change for the nation. Then, since the summer is too hot here, Habibul invited Mr. David to visit Keokradong, a beautiful peak of Bandarban, hill districts of Bangladesh, this winter. After doing some work here and perhaps having a nice holiday, they'll return.

It was a Sunday.

Idris Molla was returning from the mosque after Zohr prayer at noon. His piety led him to pray five times a day. He has a pretty simple appearance. It is always a white punjabi with matching pyjamas that he wears. He has a dark long beard but no moustache, and he is bold.

He met Habibul Islam and David Craft on his way home.

“Assalamu Alaikum, Mr. Idris.” Habibul greeted Idris.

“Walaikum Assalam Habibul.” Idris Molla smiled broadly. “I heard you were back home, but I was unable to meet up with you.”

“I understand. Is everything going well for you?” In a polite manner, Habibul inquired. As Mr. David does not understand Bengali, he was curious about what the two were talking about.

“It would be nice if I could say that I am doing well.” Idris mumbled these words to himself. “But anyway… where are you going?”

“Not anywhere in particular. We are walking around a bit... Please meet Professor David Craft. He is my colleague at the university in London where I teach.”

“Oh really? That’s nice!” Idris Molla smiled at Mr. David and the latter held out one of his hands to shake hands.

Idris Molla shook David's hands with both hands and explained in Bengali, "Keokradong welcomes you! Every indigenous family here is very friendly. We will be happy to help you with anything you might need while you are here."

"David doesn't speak Bengali, uncle."

"Oh! Habibul, if you can translate for me, that would be great! Let's go to my place, we will talk there."

"Maybe another time, uncle?" Habib was a bit reluctant.

"Hey! I'm not taking no for an answer! The people around this place have changed too much. It used to be a big celebration if someone returned from abroad. They were invited over for dinner by relatives as often as possible just to enjoy themselves. Now it seems that no one cares…"

"It's not that uncle!" Habib apologised awkwardly. "It would be nice to go to your house. Let's do that."

"Yes, let's go." Idris Molla smiled and looked at David. "Mr. David! Please excuse me, but I just can't let you guys go without having a little nap at my house. Habibul's aunt, my wife, makes really good chai tea! It's worth a try."

Habibul translated this for Mr. David.

David feels glad to be in such a welcoming situation. He found Idris Molla to be quite nice.

Idris Molla's house was just around the corner, so they all started walking towards it together.

As David walked, he noticed Idris's stress level from his manner, even though he wasn't quite sure what Habibul and Idris Molla were talking about. There was no doubt that the man needed some rest.

Lunch was served at Idris Molla's house.

Afterwards, aunt's fresh chai was fantastic!

Having received such generous hospitality, Muhammad Habibul Islam and David Craft were pleased when they left. The afternoon at Idris Molla's house was out of the blue, but it ended up being a relaxing one for them.

#

The room that people call a guest room in town is usually known as a 'bungalow-room' in a village. It has two purposes - guest room and sitting-room.

The room David Craft occupied was one of these. There was a lot of ventilation in the room.

When Mr. David returned from Idris Molla's house, he laid down on his bed. A painful headache started making his forehead throb. In his head, this one line was reverberating what Habibul explained to him- *The guy we had lunch with was the employer of the two murdered men.*

"Oh! So that's why he was so tense?" David asked Habibul.

"Who? Idris uncle? No. I don't think so. Those two were really awful men. It's a good thing they're gone!" Habibul is writing something down in his note. "In my opinion, it isn't that strange. I'm sure they messed with some people that shouldn't have been messed with."

"Maybe… Is this kind of thing common here?"

"It is not uncommon for robberies to take place, but this is the first time these murders have taken place, as far as I know... well… actually seven years ago, something happened here. I was already in London when I heard that an indigenous woman had been abused. She was not given justice by the villagers; rather, she was expelled from the village for being a member of the local drama group. There was no police case filled because she was considered a witch. I don't think there have been any crimes since then."

"What a strange thing! A woman got abused and

nobody did anything! Now two men die and no one intervenes." David Craft said with shock.

"Don't be so surprised, David. Hundreds of women get abused in our country every day. And dozens of murders are a quite simple issue."

David didn't seem to be comfortable at all. Although it was not cold, his bad headache soon became so painful that he covered himself with a blanket. A few chores needed to be done in the house, so Habibul went inside.

Few minutes after dusk, the entire sky was covered with clouds. An ominous atmosphere was created by the darkness and the clouds. There was a strong sense that a heavy storm was on its way.

As David's headache gets worse, it becomes increasingly unbearable, uncanny.

#

The time is now 9 p.m. That's really late for a village like Keokradong. There was quite a lot of wind when the storm started.

Idris Molla was counting Tasbih in his room. Islamic dhikr, *Tasbih*, involves praise of Allah by saying *Subhan Allah*. Idris Molla didn't seem to be bothered by the storm at all. After Magrib prayer, he lay on the bed relaxing, not thinking of anything.

Aleya entered the room. She was followed by Rozina holding a cup of tea. Except for Idris, his wife Mosammat Aleya Begum and the maid Rozina, no one else lived in this house.

Rozina passed the tea cup to Idris and left.

“Rozina mentioned a foreigner she saw with Habibul today.”Aleya asked, wondering if Habibul had brought a foreigner guest with him.

Idris was quite annoyed. “What nonsense! Didn’t you notice who was here for lunch today?” he asked.

“I’m sorry. I didn’t approach them, and you didn’t tell me anything.” She replied as though she had made a mistake by showing her curiosity.

“Why would you even care? ”

“Well, Mr. Habib’s return reminded me of something.”

“What?!”

“Khairun, the girl from the drama group... weren’t they in a relationship…”

“Would you mind shutting up for a moment? What is the point of bringing up such old stories? ”

“Well, didn’t Habibul tried to file a case with the police?”

“That is ancient history now and you need to shut up,” said Idris as he got off the bed. He always talked like this to his wife knowing she wouldn't mind.

"Where are you going?" Aleya wanted to know.

"I need to go to the toilet. Give me a lamp."

"Is it absolutely necessary to go out in such a storm?"

"Arrrghhhh…" Idris looked annoyed beyond measure.

Aleya handed Idris a lamp, wondering why he seemed so agitated. She always makes him irritated by asking "nonsense" questions. Idris thinks her questions sound like she simply doesn't understand anything but wants to know all the details.

The toilet was located at a distance from the house, under a betel nut tree which was located near the pond and a short walk from the house. To get to it, Idris had to walk along a narrow path.

Idris Molla went outside with the lamp but before going out, he placed the tasbih on his wife's neck like a necklace.

He knows that his wife asks many questions because she is innocent-minded. It is not every question that makes Idris Molla so irritated as it is now. So, before Aleya could ask him anymore questions, he stepped outside!

#

Somewhere nearby, there was a flash of lightning that could be seen. There was a loud noise that caused Professor David Craft to wake up from his sleep.

It was dark in the room and there was a candle burning.

Without a doubt, there was a problem with the electricity.

The majority of houses in Keokradong were equipped with electricity. Palli Bidyut supplied power. Even though the monthly bill was quite low, there were multiple blackouts every day. Each time the electricity would remain off for at least an hour. Now that there was a storm, it was inevitable.

It took David Craft a few moments to find his way back to reality after waking up so suddenly. While lying in bed, he thought about his day.

He suddenly felt his head ache again. There was an increase in swelling on his forehead.

It became apparent to David that someone or something had possessed him. Having happened three times already, this was the third instance. The first time was in the morning, and the second time was at noon.

"You're back, aren't you?" David asked to the invisible figure in the room.

He heard a female voice inside his head say, "Don't be afraid, it's the last time."

"What do you want from me?"

"Nothing. Something needs to be taken care of."

"But who are you?"

"If you believe with certainty that I'm inside you right now, I'll tell you. But do you think that I'm in your head? "

"Yes, I do."

"Good. Since I cannot do what I want until you believe I exist, I needed to be sure."

"What do you want to do?"

"As soon as the timing is right, you'll know. In the meantime, I want to use you for a while."

"How are you able to speak my language? "

"Because I'm inside your mind. No matter what language you speak, I will be able to reciprocate in the same language. I am controlling your brain."

"What's your name?"

"Khairun…"

"What? Say that again!"

"My name is Khairun. Seven years ago the people of this village banished me. There was nowhere for me to go. My solution was to jump under a train."

In a state of shock, David Craft could not speak. In the middle of the storm, only the sound of the wind could be heard.

"My search for a virtuous man has gone on for a long time, and you seem to be that man. First, I used you to enter the village, but after sending you and Habibul out, I used you as my first step. Through you, I managed to kill those two Vagabonds..." The women inside David's brain uttered these words all at the same time like a machine without emotion.

"What exactly are you talking about? "

"Do you honestly think you went to the town? Can you remember it? You can't, can you? You were busy killing those two men."

"Are you referring to Idris Molla's employees? "

"Yes. They abducted me. That fateful night, how can I ever forget it? "

"What happened that night?"

"Idris Molla and his workers raped me. I screamed and begged for mercy, but to no avail. It was a stormy night, just like tonight. They didn't show me any mercy; neither will I show any to them."

"I believe you. What are you going to do now?"

"Get up! You need to go now. It's time."

The voice faded away. David Craft stood up, hypnotised. In the direction of the door, he moved forward. There was no flame left on the candle. Candles burned out.

#

Boom! There was a sound like an explosion when the thunder rolled! A disastrous storm had swept through the area the previous night. Branches of betel nut trees were floating in the pond. The roofs of certain houses had been blown off and were scattered here and there.

People from all the surrounding villages were rushing towards Sungsawng Para. They were going to Idris Molla's house. Their attention was not drawn to the destruction that had been caused by the storm. The scream of someone echoed through the field: "What happened to Idris Molla? "

There was no response. It was an avalanche of people rushing to the house of Idris Molla to find out what had happened.

#

Several days later.

It was about time for Professor David Craft and Muhammad Habibul Islam to return to London. Earlier that morning, it was still dark. David was lying down on the bed. She came again.

"So you'll be leaving today, right?" From David's brain, she asked.

"Yes, and you're coming with me."

"That's true. You are the giver of my new life."

"Don't say that. If you don't want to, you don't have to."

"I want to. It was only thanks to you that the man survived."

"I wouldn't call it survival. You've successfully punished Idris Molla. He's a zombie now. He went insane."

"You're right. But I wish I had never joined that drama group. I wouldn't have been raped then. I could have died a peaceful death."

"A woman's body has the power to turn a pious man like Idris Molla into a demon. His genuineness is unknown to me, but the evil forced him to bow down in front of a woman's beauty."

"I forgive him. My soul is at peace now. Thank

you, David."

"No, rather I should thank you. I learnt a valuable lesson from all this."

"I believe you will keep your faith."

"I will remember you forever, Khairun."

"And I will be there for you."

The two of them kept talking. As if they had known each other forever. On the other side of the village, at Idris Molla's house, lying down speechless, shocked, and frightened, Idris Molla was completely paralysed, but still aware of what had happened!

It is still hard for him to believe what he saw before the thunder struck!

———

A Haunting Story

THE FIRST BODY

On the third day of the week, I found Frederick dead in my house. On the fourth day, my chauffeur Ahmod was killed in a car accident. My wife choked to death on the fifth day after something stuck in her throat and suffocated her. In the sixth day, Rezia, my wife's younger sister, died from stab wounds.

On the first day, who died?

It's hard for me to remember, but I'll tell you as soon as I do.

Frederick was a childhood friend of mine. How did he die? The answer is *I don't know!* It was a pleasure to have him as my family doctor. My x-ray report was next to his dead body that day. I have been feeling pain in my chest for the last few weeks, so perhaps he came to give me the report. I had prayed right on time as usual that evening as whenever I pray, I do so on time, five times a day. It's never been an issue for me to let anything stop me. Alhamdulillah. I usually perform salat at home since my bungalow is very far from the town and the nearest mosque is about five miles away. My ritual is to wait for each prayer and make myself ready just before the muezzin announces Adan. Normally when the time for salat comes, my living room has a nice wall clock that does the muezzin's job. A beautiful voice announces the Adan. It would be a dream come true for me to announce Adan in such a beautiful manner! I brought that clock almost ten years ago from Turkey. Since then, it hasn't stopped.

When I returned home that evening, I saw Frederick lying on the staircase as I was about to go upstairs. It seemed as though he had passed away a few hours ago. It took me that long to get home because there was an excellent lecture being given by the Imam at the mosque. It just so happened that at the same time, the Imam was reminding us all about death. He was telling us that we should not wait for our death and should keep continue doing our duty and all good deeds. At the time, I had no idea that someone close to me was lying dead in my own house, it could have been anyone else, even me. According to my observation sense, Frederick must have seen something or someone.

You wouldn't believe it, but I didn't really care. As if nothing happened, I haven't seen anything, and everything is just as it should be. I went upstairs in a quite normal way and went to bed quite unperturbed so I could have a long sleep without any disturbance!

The following day I was surprised to see my old trusted chauffeur, Ahmod, trying run away from me! I believe he saw me from a distance, panicked, and drove onto the main highway. According to my observation sense, he must have done something wrong. Unfortunately, Ahmod was not paying attention to the huge truck coming from the other side of the road... Poor Ahmod!

Again, you may not believe, but I wasn't able to feel anything at all while I was there. But, well, it was an antic car! It was a rare car that I bought after selling my previous one. A tremendous loss, so yes, I was saddened by the loss of my car!

However, there is no doubt that, deep down, I cried a bit when I came home from town to discover my wife Rabeya choking to death. It was the fifth day of the week. I had no reaction whatsoever. She left me as the only person in the world she knew.

Rezia, my wife's only sister, was studying in America.

Rezia called me out of the blue to let me know she would be out visiting us the next day, which was a complete surprise to me. Sadly, she died shortly after arriving here. The shock of her sister's death probably made her a bit insane. I was downstairs, doing just nothing. According to my observation sense, she must have seen something or someone downstairs, taken the knife to protect herself, run inside bedroom, and may have accidentally killed herself. Her eyes were fixed on my wife's photos in the album when it happened.

The moment I heard a scream, I rushed upstairs only to find that she had stabbed herself in the neck.

What a poor thing!

The last I heard of her, she had married someone, but there was a lot of tension in the relationship and some issues were going on. She had no children. Several months later, I learned that the couple had divorced. It is a fact of life that man is mortal!

Now, I haven't told you who died on the first or second day of the week.

It doesn't matter now, I guess!

For now, let me tell you who died on the second day of the week. Although I remember who died on the first day, I don't think it would hurt to find out a bit later.

It was the first time I had seen the man who died on the second day of the week.

I was reading the newspaper in my room when this guy phoned me and said, "Sir, I'm Rafiq. I am calling from the city. Ahmod, your chauffeur, is my younger brother. If you would allow me to come over and see him at your house, I would appreciate it very much."

It did not take Rafiq more than fifteen minutes to

arrive.

I was the only one at home at the time.

Rafiq's ugly and cruel appearance genuinely scared me. When I'm scared, I go a little crazy, so I had to do something to calm myself down.

My first thought was to offer the man some tea without really thinking. He said he would. So I had the chance to get away from him for a little while. He looked like a murderer to me. I was wondering if I should call the police but by that time, my fear had subsided a bit. I called Ahmod to ask him to come home as fast as he could. He was on duty, driving my wife's car, she was visiting a friend.

As soon as they returned, I couldn't figure out what to do with Rafiq's body! I was preparing tea for us both in the kitchen. Poor Rafiq died while he was just sitting in the living room. According to my observation sense, he must have seen something or someone on the stairs, his eyes were fixed.

The whole experience terrified me, but I didn't tell anyone.

I didn't even tell Ahmod because he would have been very lost. Telling anyone else was out of the question.

I hid Rafiq's corpse. That was the best thing to

do, wasn't it?

I'm sure you are thinking that I'm about to tell you who died on the seventh day, aren't you? Fortunately, no one died on that day.

I would say not yet at least, since today is the seventh day of the week!

The dead bodies were dumped in the basement because I didn't know what to do with them all, and I didn't want to scare anyone.

#

It is said that the only dirt rich people have on their hands is money. The way they spend their money makes it look, sound, and feel like dust, which they wipe up without thinking.

In my opinion, it would be quite unusual for them to have ever been involved in some other form of 'dirt' dealing, especially something as serious as murder. It is still possible, however, that one day or another, murder can just become another kind of dirt on their hands!

Although Mr. Mostofa did not need money, killing could still be a very simple task for him. He had given me the impression that way from the story he had been telling me. In describing the five abnormal deaths in seven days, he spoke as if they were ordinary events. But for murder to occur, a motive must exist.

I was quite relaxed and decided to light a cigar. I offered one to Mr. Mostofa as well.

He refused.

The bungalow he was living in was luxurious. A quiet atmosphere permeated the house. It was impossible to find another house within a five-mile radius. A house such as this would only be built by a very refined person if he was living in a very secluded area.

It seemed that Mr. Mostofa wasn't as refined as he appeared. There was nothing fancy about the sitting room. I could see there was nothing more to it than a few pieces of quite simple furniture. There's also that huge clock on the wall.

There were a lot of holes in the story that the man told.

"Since today is the seventh day of the week," I asked him, "Do you have anyone left at your house to die? "

Mr. Mostofa was wearing lungi and a shirt. He didn't even look at me, just looked at the ceiling. "There is no one else in this house right now except for you," he said simply.

There was no reaction on my part. "In other words, you mean that I am the one going to die tonight, aren't you?..."

"Maybe. But I hope you have noticed that everyone who has died so far was someone I knew or someone related to one of my acquaintances. You are not any of those," he said.

"That's true. It's not as if you're directly responsible for their deaths, despite the fact that you seem indifferent to them," I reasoned. "Tell me something - so many people died and yet you don't seem to care. You didn't even call the police. Could it be that you actually killed them? Though you don't mention it, you seem to be trying to show that you have some mental abnormality. What exactly are you trying to prove?"

Shaking his head, Mr. Mostofa sighed. "I'd be called a murder suspect if I was reported to the police, but where is the murder here?" he asked.

"Well, you might not consider it murder, but to me it seems like murder..." There is a bit of temper in me right now. "What about Frederick? Was he suffering from any health issues? As you just buried them all under the basement without reporting it to anyone, we will never know the reason for their deaths! How can a man who was completely healthy just die? If Rafiq and Ahmod's deaths were accidents, wouldn't you want to know how your wife got choked to death? And as for Rezia, she didn't usually walk around with a knife, did she? And please don't tell me that you keep knife in your bedroom!"

I paused after this long diatribe.

By then, I was irritated with myself.

When a man becomes annoyed, he is likely to become angry as well. I wasn't angry, but just irritated because I had a problem of my own.

It was right outside this house that my car broke down. The weather was cold and windy outside, and I didn't have any warm clothes on. It is hard to predict how the night would have gone for me if this man had not helped me out.

But now I was having second thoughts...

Over four hours had already passed since I arrived. I could have been at home performing the Tahajjud prayer and sipping hot tea, but no!

During the four hours I was stuck with the insane man. It was apparent that he lived alone. But if he was insane, how could he manage all by himself? I had the impression that he was a logical and realistic person. As I pondered what to do, I became more confused.

There was a lot of confusion in my mind.

"Mr. Iftekhar!" Mr. Mostofa addressed me by my name, which in our four-hour acquaintance was the only thing he knew about me, "You do not believe all what I just told you. It seems to you that I am a lunatic. Come on, take a look for yourself! "

That was when I started feeling cold, although the room was quite warm.

I stood up slowly.

My eyes were fixed on his face, trying to determine whether he was joking or not. But Mr. Mostofa approached me and grabbed me by the hand.

It was a cold hand with bony fingers.

He dragged me across the room.

I was wondering if there were really five corpses lying somewhere in this dark house.

Burning eyes filled Mr. Mostofa's face. It was likely that he could see everything through the darkness of the night.

#

There is one hour left until midnight. The seventh day of the week was about to come to an end. There is a possibility that someone will die tonight as well, especially since people have been dying all week. Take Mr. Iftekhar for instance. The man was sweating in such cold weather. One could read his exact thoughts from just looking at his face. It seemed as though he was compelled to believe everything I said. Although he appeared nervous, he seemed to be in control and calm. He made me feel a greater sense of respect for him. Although for a moment down there when he saw those corpses, he was suspecting me as the killer. But he was quite an intelligent man and agreed with me quite fast. There was one shocking tendency in him that I just noticed. In such a situation it was only normal for him to try and escape from this house but instead he started planning how to get rid of the bodies! Weird world and strange people!

"Mr. Iftekhar, we can't stay awake the whole night like this. It's too cold outside. The other rooms don't have heater but my bedroom has one. If you want you can spend the night there", I said to Mr. Iftekhar.

"Thanks a lot but I don't want you out of my sight", said Mr. Iftekhar, looking at me.

"Why? Do you think there is a third person in the house, considering I am not the killer?"

"No, that's not what I'm thinking at all. I just want to test something out. I want to see if you try to do anything, considering you in fact are the killer."

"Mr. Iftekhar, I tell you again, these can't be murders. I admit, the deaths are quite abnormal but…okay, tell me, why are you thinking that way?"

"If you in fact are the killer, then you are a serial killer and you will try to kill me just to maintain your seven-day roll".

"There must be a motive to kill someone, right?"

"There probably is one. I'm trying to figure out what that might be."

I was quite amazed at Mr. Iftekhar's intellect. The first thing I need to know about him is who he is and what he does for a living.

"Mr. Iftekhar, do tell, who are you actually? And what is your occupation?"

"So, now you are interested in knowing more about me, huh?" Mr. Iftekhar mocked me.

“Anyway, I won’t lie to you. I am an Imam.”

This information should have made me nervous but it didn’t. Well, there was nothing to be nervous about. I didn’t do anything. But of course, I was quite surprised.

“I am shocked that if you are Mr. Mostofa, why didn’t you recognise me when I saw you often in the mosque?” Mr. Iftekhar looked at me as if he could see me through my eyes! He pulled a bottle from his pocket. That bottle contains some clear water. Maybe Mr. Iftekhar feels trusty and wants to drink some water.

He looks at me strangely, but why?

Mr. Iftekhar threw me some water from the bottle before I could doubt anything! As I screamed out so loud, even hearing my own scream frightened me! It was terrifying and unearthly. My mind suddenly flashed back to the person who died on the first day of the week!

#

After leaving Mr. Mostofa’s house, Mr. Iftekhar came to the mosque a few hours later.

It is almost Fajr time. There are many Musallies in mosques. All eyes were on Imam Iftekhar. A speech is about to be delivered by him. Standing up, he adjusted his mic and looked around the room. Then he gave salam to everyone, and everyone replied.

"Over the last few years," Mr. Iftekhar started, "I have been serving as the Imam of this only mosque. Even though I don't personally know every Musalli who comes to perform salat, I recognise them by their faces. In my spiritual lectures, I used to notice Mr. Mostofa attending. Mr. Mostofa is the only person who lives quite far from us since he built his house to be a little away from the crowd. We all know the place on which his house was built was cursed and once belonged to Jinns…" As the whispering began, Mr. Iftekhar was interrupted. "The problem is that we never pay attention to it. Today, I was on my way home via the land of Mr. Mostofa. My car broke down near his house, so I was glad to be greeted by Mr. Mostofa himself. Only after our conversation and the strange behaviour that Mr. Mostofa showed did I realise he had actually been struck by black magic and was even possessed by a Jinn. Not for a single second did he recognise me. Upon gaining control of the situation, I found six dead bodies, one of which was Mr. Mostofa and his wife…His house was full of evidence and signs of Voodoo, and I believe one of these people wanted to harm Mr. Mostofa. Maybe they also called out the jinn or it was done by mistake. Mr. Mostofa himself was killed first, and then one by one the others were killed. I found this to be the most mysterious issue I encountered."

Whisper is now being spread throughout the mosque. Some people stand up in fear, some try to clam themselves down. Everyone recites *Inna lillahi wa inna ilayhi raji'un* out loud.

As he continued his sermon, Imam Mr. Iftekhar recited it loudly with the meaning, "*Indeed, we belong to Allah, and indeed, to Him we return.*"

Suddenly, the entrance door opened with a loud crack.

Everyone looked in that direction.

Six coffins are brought inside the mosque by police and volunteers. Everybody stands up as a sign of respect, even in the midst of great confusion and fear. Continuing, Imam Mr. Iftekhar said- "therefore, I abrogate the land of Mr. Mostofa as abandoned, haunted, and request no one should buy it or pass by until an investigation is conducted by the authorities. We will perform the Fajr salat as usual after the Fajr Adan, and then we will conduct

Janaza salat for Mr. Mostofa and everyone who passed away. In a Hadith, prophet Muhammad (PBUH) states that satan flees to a distant place when he hears the call to prayer, the Adan…"

Adan has been announced. The message didn't reach Mr. Mostofa's house, which is far from the mosque.

#

A few weeks earlier. The afternoon was sunny on Saturday.

It had just been a few minutes since Mr. Mostofa had left the chamber of his doctor friend Frederick. The purpose of his visit was to hand over some recent photos and to go through some routine checkups as Frederick requested. As soon as Frederick had made sure that Mostofa was gone and out of sight, he dialled a telephone number.

"Rezia, he's in good health. I can't fake routine check like this. He might start doubting. Now you have to act." Frederick exclaimed.

Rezia, Mr. Mostofa's sister-in-law, spoke up- "Have you been able to collect the materials? Send me his up-to-date photo and hair. I've found a Voodoo guy who can handle the rest."

They continued talking where Rezia elaborated and made a plan like this: Rabeya with Ahmod's help will sacrifice something to start the process. Rafiq, a Voodoo priest, will somehow make his way into the house to meet Mr. Mostofa, since the mantra will need to be blown in order to make the ritual work. He may use the photos and hair to conduct the remote session if this isn't possible. It will only take a few days once everything is in place for them to take control of the land and conquer the Jinns living within.

The two were very confident that their plan would work. They believe that the evil spirit lives within Mr. Mostofa.

If they take control over Mostofa, they may be able to control that jinn. But they both were unaware that Mr. Mostofa was not possessed by anything harming him because he avoided thinking of harming anyone or anything.

Both of them were also unaware that there was something in Frederick's chamber that day that was invisible, out of sight, but enraged with a smokeless flame. It was listening in on their conversation, all the while, unnoticed!

STRANGE SERIOUS SHORT STORIES SsSs...

Some Terrific Tales

Illustrations by **Anna Oloffson**

AUTHOR'S NOTE
Thank you so much for finishing the first segment. You will now enjoy my two standalone books, which are illustrated by another artist, ***Anna***. My *Strange Serious Short Stories* SsSs… are some weird short stories I wrote when I began blogging in 2009! I was kept engaged by hundreds of readers who responded non-stop! I wrote multiple stories in one sitting and replied to everyone's comments at the same time… What a memory! — ***Uncle Nafee***

PURAB'S MIRROR — A SUPERNATURAL STORY

My mobile phone was ringing when I got home that afternoon. I had just returned from playing football and was totally drenched with sweat. I answered the phone. "Hello Purab, why are you calling me?"

"Oh, hello my friend! I want you to come over to my house please."

"I've just got home after the match. If you don't

mind I'll call round a little later."

"No, no, Ritesh! Please come now."

"Purab, I'm still dressed in my sports wear…"

"Shut up and just come right now. Please!"

Purab ended the communication. He was obviously agitated.

#

"Come on. Come on!" Purab moved aside from the gate and ushered me into his house.

I entered with astonishment. "What's happened, Purab?"

Purab smiled at my flabbergasted expression.

He closed the door and gestured to me to sit down on the sofa. I didn't like what was going on and got rather annoyed.

"What's the matter?" I wanted to know what was wrong. "Is there nobody in the house?"

There was indeed nobody there.

#

I will never forget what Purab showed me. It was quite amazing and still keeps me awake at night!

He told me to look at his eyes.

I did so, and saw that they were transparent.

Then I stood up and Purab was no longer in front of me. The person standing opposite me was myself - Ritesh!

Purab told me that from now on people would not need mirrors. If anybody wanted to see him or herself, they would just have to look at the eyes of another person for few seconds and they will find themselves to be the other person!

I promised to Purab that I would not tell anybody about his discovery.

#

A strange idea occurred to me that night. I called Purab and asked how I could do it by myself. He taught me the process. However, he warned me that if I did it for more than three minutes, then the person who appeared before me would change into my form.

He told me to be careful.

#

I didn't try out the idea that night because I wanted to put it into practice another time. The truth is that I am in love with a girl called Rintu and I wanted to get into her house somehow.

So I befriended her younger brother and one day I compelled him to look at my eyes…

When I left, I took out my small pocket mirror and looked at myself.

I had changed into Rintu's brother!

———

UNKNOWN — AN SPOOKY STORY

The weekly paper *Srishti* is doing very well. It is distributed to many subscribers and has about ten thousands plus readers all over the country.

The editor, Noresh Huda, is an extremely skilled and capable person. He manages everything, including compiling, cover design, article selection, marketing and so on. *Srishti* is in a good position in all respects.

One day a superb story arrived by post.

Noresh Huda was astonished after reading the stories. The author name was Daud Khan.

He kept it at the top of his list for publishing in the upcoming issue. Noresh couldn't remember whether the writer had sent in any story before, so he presumed he must be new. There was no address with the story. It was explicitly mentioned in brackets that the sender was unwilling to give his contact details.

Noresh Huda assumed that the writer has come to shake the world! Here's how one of the story were written:

Story 1: ***THE YARD***

It was a new house.

There was a broad space in front of the house and huge bushes on either side. It would be incredible to get any trees with scented flowers to grow there. However, Zafar worked hard all day to completely clean the place up and then he ordered some seedlings from a nursery. They were due to arrive the following morning.

Next day, Zafar dug a place to sow the seedlings,

hoping that one day they would grow into saplings and eventually produce flowers.

But suddenly, as he dug, a rotten, disintegrated, worm-eaten hand came out of the hole!

Zafar could not stop himself from vomiting.

However, he managed to control himself, but stood aghast as he watched all the different parts of a man's body emerging one by one from the cavity.

Zafar dug a grave in his yard, but couldn't decide whether he should call the police.

That day, from the roof of a building on the other side of the road, another person was watching what Zafar was doing.

The mysterious man laughed at Zafar in a disdainful manner, then moved away.

He was the man who had killed the person and had been waiting for someone to discover the body so that this story could begin!

What a story!

Noresh Huda published the story on the following issue of *Srishti* on schedule.

#

Few weeks passed.

It was one afternoon when Noresh Huda sat in his office with the manager, Gupta, to chat.

He browsed through the paper and discussed the new contributions.

A man dressed in a suit and overcoat was also there…

The guest introduced himself as the grandson whose one anonymous story, *THE YARD*, had been published in the paper. He had come to find out where *Srishti* got the story from. As the guest confirmed, the author was his grandfather, who passed away more than thirty years ago. They own their grandfather's manuscripts, have read them many times and so they are familiar with the story *Srishti* published.

At his request, they all went out and gathered under an ancient banyan tree.

There was a grave beside the tree.

The headstone showed that the name of the dead man was the writer *Daud Khan*!

#

Noresh Huda was working in his office some days after that incident when an envelope arrived.

He opened it to find a manuscript with a letter.

The letter read, "*All that I have written in my life is in the grave with me. I kindly request you to secure my writings.*"

Norsesh's body shook with fear.

The handwriting matched the handwriting of writer Daud Khan!

A CITY WITHOUT MONEY — A Sci-Fi Story

I had been waiting beside the bus stop for a long time.

I was a newcomer to the city.

I got there directly via the river.

I am a refuge guy.

I became a pauper after being for the dream of going to London. I did not know where my journey would end and whether I would be alive or dead. I was staying in the city whose name I had never seen on any map of the world. Yet it seemed to be ultra-modern. I felt like a kind of latter-day Robinson Crusoe!

#

The bus stopped automatically and everyone got out. It was a bus without a driver! The door opened automatically. When I heard the mechanical voice of a computer, I understood that I had to get on the bus and click a button to choose my destination. I chose my journey at random, opting for a destination called *Gonajalabad Trainipass Minensa* Station.

#

I spent no money.

I arrived at the station, which was an empty, wide field.

I sat down on a sofa. A robotic tune told me to write the name of my destination. I typed the name of my own city. It seemed that I slept for a while. When I awoke I felt a strange touch on my shoulder. Again, a mechanical tune announced that I had arrived at my destination. I got up from the sofa. Wow, I was in my own city!

#

I repeatedly tried to make someone believe this story, but to no avail. So in the end I gave up talking about it. But when I got married, I told my new bride about the incident. My wife wanted to go on our honeymoon soon after the wedding, she expressed the desire to see the mysterious city. However, she would not return immediately from the city as I had done. She wanted to wander around and explore it. Our honeymoon would be fruitful.

So I went back to that city with my wife.

There was nobody living there.

It was a lifeless, paperless city.

To get around we pressed buttons and talked into machines, but we spent absolutely no money!

———

WHEN ALL ARE IN A SINGLE CITY…

— A SCI-FI STORY

That day, as I was chilling with my friends in my flat, they all began asking me, "Ayan, why can't we see you?"

I was astonished!

What exactly did they mean when they said they couldn't see me? They can hear me, however!

I am certain that my friends are not joking.

All of my friends thought that was amusing, and they approached and even touched me. I could tell from the look on their faces that they couldn't feel my body. And I saw them vanish right in front of me as soon as they touched me!

As I stood up, I put my half-finished tea cup next to the bed and looked into the wardrobe mirror; however, no one seemed to be looking at me in the mirror. In the mirror, I don't see anyone at all!

I strolled around the city's sidewalks and streets. I was invisible, though. No one was visible to me either!

####

Once, when I got up in the morning, nobody was in the house. In fact, I stepped out without even having a cup of tea, but there was no one in the city!

As I stood alone in the middle of the street, I began to think about what had happened. In the distance, I heard a disembodied voice asked, "Is there anyone here? "

I could hear them next to me.

I could sense them. But I saw no one. Does this mean that the voices of those who have completely disappeared will no longer be heard, soon?

By now, the entire city has disappeared! As far as I can see, there is nothing visible to me.

It is silent.

My feet felt like they were floating in space, nothing beneath them, above me, or around me!

There is no sound coming from anywhere. Though it's possible that everyone is here, I can't see or hear them the way they can't see me anymore!

This does not mean that I am blind; rather, it means that I am invisible!

Then I saw them. They were visible in the distance, giving me the impression that I was floating and that everything had vanished all around me.

Actually, that's what's happening!

We're disappearing, and they're appearing!

I am certain that all of us have been caged by aliens…

—

CLONED — A SCI-FI STORY

When I enjoyed the majesty of the moon by standing beside the window, I got much pleasure, but I just don't know what happened to me today!

I feel a little different.

I was gazing up at the sky sipping on a cup of tea, I see not one moon, but two!

###

After getting up in the morning, I notice the TV is on.

I forgot to switch it off! But I can see I did not forget to finish my cup of tea!

I turned the TV off using the remote control beside my bed.

It seems wrong to get up in case I wake anyone.

So I was looking at the ceiling fan.

Abruptly I noticed there were two ceiling fans!

###

Entering the kitchen, I set the kettle on to make tea.

Then I went to the bathroom.

I observed my face standing in front of the mirror.

I threw cool water from the tap to my face.

Again, I saw the mirror.

Yes, another me stood up behind me.

There are two of me!

It seems to be that everything in the world has cloned. The world itself was certainly cloned…

####

"Watch please…" astronaut Wanky asked his captain to see the outside of their spaceship.

"Wonderful!" Someone from behind, screamed.

"Are we all watching the same thing?" Captain Tanky was amazed.

"Certainly! Which one will be the perfect entrance for us? Which one is the real one?" Captain Tanky and his co-pilot Wanky were in total confusion.

###

When a team of returning astronauts from Mars to the planet Earth saw another planet Earth besides their planet, nobody understood which one was real!

———

THE LAST SIGN — A SCI-FI STORY

'Is everything destroyed, under control?' Robot leader Ribornart asked his/its commando companion Rikoart.

"Yes." Rikoart answered.

All of them were standing in a destroyed kitchen of someone.

"What were you concerned about then?" Ribornart asked his/its commando companion again. Around them, so many broken white cups except one half finished cup of tea. However, a humanoid robot presumably cannot detect the scent of a cup of tea.

“Watch…” Rikoart pointed something using his/its wrist display device, which was connected to unlimited cameras to monitor the entire human zone.

Ribornart carefully observed every detail in the camera footage.

“Hmm... So all of them died?” Ribornart wants to know. Actually he/it wanted to whisper in the air as if he/it was a human.

“We may stay on this planet now.” Rikoart assumed.

“OK, now time to start a new world. We should give a name of this planet. Roborld instead of World, Roberth instead of Earth, Roboniverse instead of Universe… Anymore suggesting?”

###

“A… Aa… I am alive…!”

A human with his last hope. That means, there is still a hope to destroy all the robots…

###

The Robots considered humankind to be extinct. Beneath their thoughts, nevertheless, was still someone alive. However, the story cannot continue. Because the living man discovered his two hands and two legs were isolated from his body and completely smashed, deleted. There were NO materials left for him to stay alive…

###

Robot commando Ribornart and his/its companion commando robot Rikoart just realised that there was still a human alive, but by now, they also saw that the man just died.

One of the commando robots tied a flag board on the ground of planet Earth. It says- ***PLANET EATRH, FOR SALE.***

——

YELLING — A SCI-FI HORROR STORY

I have the ability to focus on what I'm creating while freezing a scene like a static image. To focus on creating something, I don't need to constantly glance at or check things. It feels like I have the ability to pause a scenario in front of me and play it backward or forward. In what way is that feasible? By now, you must have realised that I am not human! You're welcome to join me for a cup of tea…

###

My daughter opened the door when the doorbell rang. She recently turned seven. She is as fair as her mother is. Her name is Rintu.

The man who stood up at the door resembled me completely. So my daughter screamed. I was also astonished when I saw myself in front of me!

I sent Rintu to her reading room.

Her mother was not at home. She went out to get some fresh air.

I had to incorporate the copy of myself into the actual form of me and had to turn myself into the copy of me before my wife came back. I created the clone with hard work.

Now, I hid myself in a secret room of the house. I had been watching the activity of the house by attaching a CC camera to a monitor screen.

During the rest of the day, I saw Rintu or her mother never noticed anything unusual from my carbon copy! And I realised that I made the biggest mistake making my own carbon copy!

###

A week passed. I tried to convince Rintu's mother that I am her real husband and the man that I made is a clone robot. Nevertheless, She didn't pay attention to what I was saying. She saw both of us but didn't care.

Rintu came to my laboratory that night. Whispering, she told me, "Dad, Mom is cleaning the skull of her head after opening it!"

I understood that my wife had replaced her real form with a copy of herself before me!

But where did she go? How she knows my formula to make self-clones!

###

That night, in shock, I saw that they tore my daughter, Rintu, apart in front of my eyes.

The floor of the living room floated with blood.

Now fake Shohana (my wife) and fake professor Dr. Rahat was coming toward me…

###

Doctor Rahat built the solitary villa in a hilly part of the city. A deadly scream flowed from the giant villa that night. There was no one to hear that yelling. Only a flock of bats disappeared into the darkness.

And… The birth of clones started from an ordinary mistake!

———

THE NIGHT OF DEATH — A HORROR STORY

Narrated by something strange…

Night 1:

I was returning at midnight. I was very much alone. There was nobody around. Everything was empty.

Was that a cat or dog?

Yes, there was a dog.

A bareheaded dog ran by just now.

I wanted to throw my poisonous spit. However, I

restrained myself from doing so.

When I was alone at night, I intended to accomplish many strange things. I saw a thief flee after theft that night. I didn't get the chance to think about whether I will catch the man. A car came with the speed of wind and smashed the thief in front of my eyes! This is what always happens to the people when they underestimate their senses. When they never apply the things they learnt from their childhood.

Hah!

Lucky me!

Night 2:

I have eaten nothing for two days. I went out to the path but stopped searching. I have not been catching the prey well; therefore my mind is not always in good condition. I decided today I would prey on something. Hmm…

Night 3:

Recently police started guarding this place. The people of the colony are passing their days and nights with fear. Murder is happening often. Thieves are taking the opportunity. However, it is not the matter of my interest.

I think about myself. There is no chicken in the trap. There is neither a cat in the trap, either. Naturally, I am very hungry. How do I do today?

Night 4:

Brother Borun is the security guard for the colony. He had daring courage despite recent events. He bears a stick in his hand to protect him in times of danger. Three murders have occurred, so everyone is restive and stays home after dark. However, Brother Borun intends to catch the murderer. The problem is, he has no idea that he is not after any human, he is seeking me! How dare he seek me? But it's not a problem; I will meet with him today. I am very hungry...

The End:

The security guard, Borun, discovered a dangerous man-eating animal at a solitary place of the lane in the shady light of moonlight. The hirsute, dangerous animal came out from a bushy place with an unearthly roar… And that's when the ends started to end!

TYPIST — A PSYCHOLOGICAL THRILLER STORY

It is the year 1999.

I work at a publishing company.

I do the work of computer composition on a contract basis. So call, it's a typist job. The publisher gives me the responsibility. I just obey his order.

I was composing a manuscript one night.

Everybody had gone. The publisher had also gone and given me the key.

The book fair would be starting very soon.

I was managing the composition of twenty-five books alone. The work had to be finished within two months. It was in the contract. Fifty grand is a considerable amount of remuneration to sacrifice little personal things, well, sometimes. I had composed fifteen books already.

It was midnight.

There was no one but me in the entire place.

I finished my work for today.

After packing up everything, I locked the office gate and went under the dark sky. Since there were lights, I could walk. My haunted (!) flat was not far away, only a two-mile path.

The man was walking past me.

I knew the man. He was a service man. He supplied tea at my place.

His attitude was very strange.

He didn't care when I said something to him.

I didn't care much about it.

What can I do if someone doesn't respond back

when you say goodnight.

"Hey Topu, today's tea was nice... May I get more tomorrow please?" Topu looked at me as if he was going to swallow me!

###

I came to my office later tomorrow.

There was a great crowd.

I tried to discover what was wrong and found out that the dead body of the service man Topu was found.

After the investigation, the police knew that nobody left from this place very late last night but me, so they took me into custody.

Later, I went to examine the scene of the crime. At last, I understood why the man died.

I had killed him.

I was thanking him for his nice cup of tea, but he didn't care about my kindness and didn't look at me when he passed just because I am not like a BOSS or such important person to him!

He showed anger when I came to him.

Topu didn't know I was at a mental hospital for

my anger. But he paid the price since he disparaged me and called me a very low class guy.

I managed this situation in such a way so that everybody understood.

I just don't want to go back to the hospital anymore. If he hadn't made me angry, I wouldn't have done it.

Why do people make me angry? And I just don't understand why people love to show their anger!

Are they mad, like me? Actually, since the mental hospital always makes pretty nice cups of tea, I don't mind returning there!

NEED — A PSYCHOLOGICAL HORROR STORY

I'm a visionary man.

My stories are crazy and a little deformed. Let me begin.

O wait! Let me grab a cup of tea first…

*

One day I saw that my pet dog had escaped.

I knew why it escaped and the dead body of

my dog was there in my back garden when I returned home at night after finishing work.

You keep reading!

*

There was a blackout in my room.

How could I watch TV?

Actually, I know how to watch TV without electricity.

Nope, don't think I am going to use the emergency stabiliser!

But yes, I'm going to use something for sure!

*

I fed my parrot at the roof of my house. It was a strange experience.

I fed it something else!

I saw the parrot sitting down with sad feathers in the morning of a day. Look like it needs something.

Actually, I knew the reason.

So I took a 'step' so that it became happy again.

My dearest parrot got its soul again.

Ya, ya!

I know how to feed even a bird without buying pet food!

*

I have much to say regarding taking care of my everyday needs. However, I've sat you down long enough to explain you how I take care of myself.

Are you still curious?

Let me reveal!

O wait, let me grab a cup of tea first!

###

I left the room. My car was inactive in the garage. I knew what to do.

So I went to the garage and used the blood of my dog who was killed by me yesterday.

I used my dog's blood as fuel! I have to meet my all-necessary and unnecessary needs in this way...

Even with the blood of anything!

It could be humans someday…

Only one different thing I must consider as my everyday pleasure, which is always, a hot cup of tea!

———

DEWRAAJ — A MONSTER STORY

A poor farmer called Monmohan went down to the solitary River to bathe.

As he walked along the bank to find a good spot to get into the water, he came across an unexpected sight.

He was enjoying his hot tea in an old mug made out of clay, and he was whistling happily. Then a sudden shock made him drop his mug.

It was a human leg!

There was blood on the leg, all dry and clotted.

Monmohan surely a brave man and not one to be easily frightened, but he was nevertheless very surprised at this discovery.

Monmohan picked up the leg and hoisted it onto his shoulder to take it home.

He lived in an isolated part of the village where nobody went very often— although sometimes people went there to see if he was available for work as Monmohan often had to go to the village market to find work.

Monmohan knew everything about the village, including all the local legends.

There was one particular myth about a creature that supposedly lived in the river. People recounted that if anybody went down to the river at midday, this monster would catch hold of one of their legs and drag them down to the bottom of the river. However, Monmohan had never found out whether this was true or not because he bathed in the river every day and had never witnessed any such occurrence. In fact, when he thought about it, he found it quite amusing.

###

There was a broken-down, abandoned temple near where Monmohan lived. He took the detached leg there and put some dry *Cadamba* (Burflower) flowers on it. He sketched a circle with sand around the leg and sat down to worship.

There was a brisk breeze blowing from the south...

###

Motlob Shet and his gang turned up at Monmohan's house in the evening.

Monmohan had eaten the leg already.

Motlob and his gang found it difficult to understand, but they were very excited for some reasons.

Motlob Shet told Monmohan, "Mohan, we threw the robber Mujib into your river last night to feed the monster. Now the police are here in the village. So I want to hide my boys at your hut for a few days. Is that any problem?"

Poor Monmohan hesitated slightly.

He knows Motlob Shet is not looking for his permission. He's not even asking. This guy is dangerous enough to kill and vanish Monmohan without leaving any clue to anyone.

Finally, Monmohan said, "That is no problem at all…Master!" Motlob Shet acted like a chivalrous knight, but he certainly had some murderous followers.

###

Next day, Monmohan was not at home. One of Motlob Shet's gang members, Vijay, who was staying in Monmohan's house, went down to the river to bathe. He was a robber and therefore not accustomed to fear.

Vijay went down to the river naked, feeling carefree. *How lovely and cool the water is…* he thought to himself. He simply doesn't care where the corpse of robber Mujib, whom they dumped in this river, is…

###

Just before his death, Vijay knew what it was to experience fear. He felt his leg being held tightly, as if in a vice, and his whole body was being dragged down to the bottom of the river.

In the final seconds before he drowned, he discovered that there really was something under the water and that the something was Monmohan!

Monmohan no longer resembles a human being; he had turned into a savage monster, and he was pulling Vijay down into the depths of the river to eat...

---

* *Dewraaj* means King of Monsters in English.

AFTER THE END — A SUPERNATURAL WESTERN STORY

The intensity of the sun's heat became unbearable.

Cowboy Oliver knew that although it was intensely hot, rain must be on the way.

He doubled his speed by holding onto the horse's reins tightly. If he could not reach Pink City within an hour, he might get soaked.

Two stray dogs ran away barking across the dusty road.

If there are people around, they would wonder how Oliver gulps down his flask full of tea while riding the horse! But Oliver is an expert having tea while on the horse.

A few horseback riders disappeared into the lane at high speed.

The intensity of heat lessened and dark clouds covered the blue sky.

The people were scared and they all closed their shops. They closed the doors and windows of their homes, and then huddled inside.

Something strange is about to happen.

###

The Pink City transformed into a silent dead city. It seemed that there was no sign of living people for hundreds of years! When the rain showered the soil drop by drop, Oliver's whole body was shaking with fear. Pink City was a hundred yards away. Oh God! If he was able to reach it anyhow...

###

After two hours, the people of Pink City slowly became active again. Everyone resumed his and her work. The city woke up. The trend of business and daily activity continued as it was before. The fear vanished.

###

Acid rain stopped!

The Pink City suffered the curses each week. If any animal was victim to this rain, its whole body burned until only the bones remained.

Oliver was able to take shelter under his quick built tent before a shower came. There was less amount of space to fit the horse. Oliver could not save even the dearest horse at any cost.

Oliver saw the death of a meek horse that was intensely frightened from the tent during heavy showers. He saw the difference between his tear and acid rain; His tear-drop burned his heart as if acid drop rolled on his cheeks…

—

DISEASE — A PSYCHOLOGICAL HORROR STORY

I wanted to convince everybody that I am going to be mad! However, nobody cared.

You may hear two events of my mental disorder-

One night I woke up suddenly.

I was extremely thirsty. But I don't drink cold

water to quench my thirst.

What did I do?

Suddenly I realised that there is hot water in the kitchen! If I went there, I would get my hot water to have a few cups of tea to quench my thirst!

However, I was not eager to go there.

What did I do, again?

Do you want to know?

It's funny but I thought under my bed a strange animal would eat my legs, so I got out of bed and rushed to the kitchen! Sometimes the best way to end idleness is to instil terror.

If you hear the second reason, you will laugh. I was supposed to go to one of my friend's houses in the morning.

I went to my mother to get some money. Mum reproached me so much that I was surprised! Mum was rebuking me but I kept silent (normally I am opposite). Everyone knew at this house that I always became so upset when my mum shouts at me.

This time I laughed and massaged the palm of my hand.

Mum began to scream.

She began to knock everybody to see the matter by saying, “Tirmij didn’t show anger!”

I went to my younger brother to know the reason for this event.

I asked what the matter was.

He rebuked me and said that I should have cried like I usually did.

I was surprised!

I didn’t recognise myself in character!

###

You may also hear a supreme event of my mental disorder.

So, the event was:

I stayed in the same room with my younger brother, where he studied at a small table.

One day there was nobody at home.

My brother was busy studying.

I was very hungry at that time.

What did I do?

There was no cooked food.

I wished to cook my younger brother after

cutting his body!

That was a strange feeling!

I was worried about how I would accomplish the feat.

Suddenly I had a way.

But I really need a hot cup of tea first!

###

Everybody came back home at noon.

My younger brother was missing.

Nobody found him after searching for two nights. They called the police through to investigate the matter…

I told everybody by yelling that I ate my younger brother.

Who believed what I said?

Nobody paid attention to me thinking I was grieving. Haven't I become mad?

Hah!

GHOSTLAND VABANPUR — A SCARY STORY

He can see everything through his binoculars. However, he saw nothing when he put it down!

Archaeologist Romon Pindu found an invisible island situated only one mile away from the high hillock of the pathless forest named Vabanpur.

Nobody can see the island with naked eyes, but when the binoculars are held in front of eyes the island is only some yards away!

Romon Pindu felt a world conqueror's joy after examining the matter several times.

He prepared himself a brilliant, warm cup of tea.

Romon Pindu always makes sure that he keeps hot tea in his flask, ready to quench his craving.

While looking through the binoculars and keeping an eye out for the island, Romon Pindu slurps mouthfuls of tea.

Did anybody else know the matter?

He had discovered the Mirin civilisation, which vanished many years ago.

There was nobody to know the great discovery of Romon Pindu from one side of Vabanpur to the farthest southern side. However, Romon Pindu became slightly alarmed about the matter.

The island was completely obvious with binoculars but totally invisible with naked eyes!

What a strange thing!

Romon sat down on a raft and began to row to the unknown mysterious Mirin civilisation.

It was difficult to row the raft. He had to hold the binoculars in front of his eyes at all times!

Romon saw that the island was coming nearer to him.

His pleasure spread.

At last he was able to anchor.

He tried to determine how far he came.

He looked at the hillock of Vabanpur…but… nothing was there!

There were only waves all around.

Astonished, Romon Pindu found himself in the central point of flowing water on a fallow solitary island of the Mirin civilisation.

He stood as the last existence of his life…

###

Romon Pindu remembered that a mysterious man told him at the path of Vabanpur, "Don't go there. Nobody comes back from the Ghost land Vabanpur!"

PULSIRAT — A HAUNTING STORY

It was a dark night. Not the residents of the earth, only the residents of this broken city; all are in profound sleep…

It is very high, like a 1000-story apartment. One is on one side and another is on the other side. A very narrow rope bridge reaches from one side to another side. To me, it's a very tiny sharp thread.

It was night, but a mysterious impression of light spread throughout the world.

The narrow thread was very clear in the mystery of illusion. It was black and feels very sharp; sharp enough to cut anything that touched it.

I stood on one leg in the middle of that sharp thread. My other leg was twisting and turning as I tried to keep my balance 1000-storeys above the ground.

I would die young if I fell down.

It was becoming impossible for me to stand up on the abnormally fine yarn. It wasn't cutting my leg, but it felt that way.

There was a blank space where my foot once was. I was very afraid when I saw that my leg was not bleeding.

How did I get here?

Why did I come to the middle of this thread drawn between two buildings at midnight?

I gave up thinking.

Then suddenly I thought I must get to the other side. Otherwise, it was certain death.

But I didn't manage to do anything. What would happen to me? Was I going to fall down?

Then I woke up.

I discovered that I was an insignificant resident of a city in a very normal environment.

It was a dark night. There was no sound anywhere, so I lay down again.

But I knew an uncertain bondage had trapped my life.

I am the last point of this bondage… it's a loop, a loop that we all scared of! Pulisirat, those who are believers can pass through that bridge without fear, so I wonder, will I be considered a true believer?

The nightmare has begun again!

---

* *Pulsirat* means *As-Sirāt*, according to Islam, the bridge over which every person must pass on the Yawm al-Qiyamah in order to enter Jannah, the paradise.

SATAN — AN SPIRITUAL TALE

Mehrab:

Mehrab Ajij was returning home after finishing his final Friday prayers. He was wearing a white hat on his head. His body was covered with a long white tub and plain white trousers. He was a holy man with a shining face. He never had sinned when he was young, then he got married. Now his life is coming to an end, letting him depart this life and go to heaven. However, a dark shadow is trying its hardest to make him sin!

Satan

I was behind the man forever! I watched him be born and passed by all his life long. However, the never committed a sin! His wife had died after ten years of marriage and no baby had been born during that time. I thought he would marry again, but he gave no sign of doing so. I have no time to wait.

Mehrab

Mehrab Ajij married when he was twenty-four years old. His wife died ten years after the marriage.

No child born during those ten years.

He had no parents, sister or brother in his earthly life.

Mehrab Ajij was an orphan, a fact he discovered only when he had grown up. His wife was also came from an orphanage. They had met and got married.

It was then they encountered an extreme satanic force and their life was never easy to lead. They kept sparing no effort to stay away from alcohol, lying, and distractions from haram things.

Satan

I can't mislead this man!

I don't know how to trick him.

There is no way to get into his mind. Nor is it possible to set up someone else as his bad wisher to curse him forever.

I now realise that he's about to die.

It was I who induced him to pursue lust and debauchery. But he never made a mistake. On top, the girl spoilt everything. They got married right after they liked each other.

I have kept following him, but without success. I can't convince either of them to commit any misdeed.

In the end, I always end up suffocating when someone doesn't do what I want them to do, but they will reap rewards here and after, and I will not even die here until the end of the world.

Mehrab & Satan

It is possible that Mehrab Ajij will not live.

He is being treated in hospital, but the doctors have given up all hope of saving him.

His wife was in the same hospital bed when she passed away, and he was beside her helpless. He felt Satan behind him, trying to make her commit a sin by accepting him as her God, but she died thirsty.

Now Mehrab's time is up.

As he drew his final breath on his hospital bed, Mehrab Ajij saw a poor soul screaming in sorrow and pain.

This evil spirit tried to confess to him that he was his creator.

So although Mehrab Ajij died, he understood that he was able to defeat the accursed Satan at all times, even at the end his life!

———

SAME AS HER — *A SCI-FI MYSTERY*

Poma saw a girl and a boy who probably lived in the house next to hers. They started to run towards the field where, a huge banyan tree stands with its branches spreading its shade all around.

Another girl from another flat also saw a girl and a boy running on the street towards the field.

Poma was on her balcony that afternoon with her

hot cup of tea when she discovered a gathering of boys and girls, again! All the girls look familiar to her.

Seeing them, this time Poma ran through the door as well…

The whole town was soon full of girls and boys who looked completely alike.

Poma discovered to her surprise that all of the girls looked exactly like her!

Or was it that she looked exactly like them?

—

ODD MAN OUT

This western novella revolves around an imaginary place called *Greentown* in the Wild West and the sudden and unexpected incidents that happened there. It was written long ago by a great fan of western fiction. It's Me, *Nafee*!

When reading Western paperbacks, I thought I would try writing one myself. I was only sixteen that time. I dreamed that one day it would publish and eventually this one appeared as a novella in a special edition of a weekly national magazine, after some rejections from other publications.

Happy reading!

Uncle Nafee

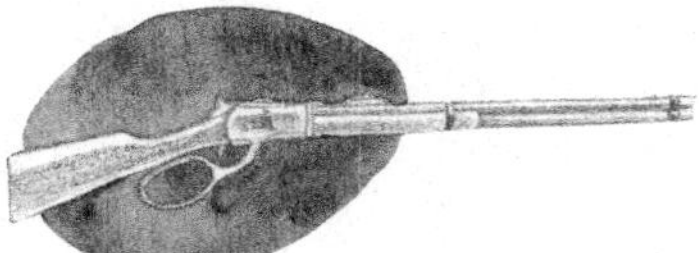

Illustrations by **Anna Oloffson**

CHAPTER 1

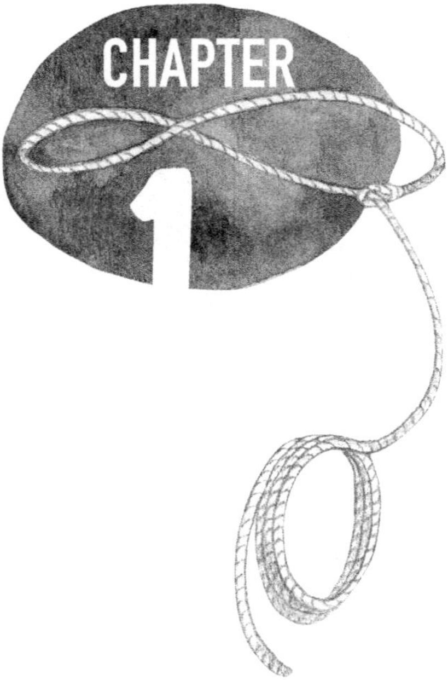

Martin was walking down the street when he suddenly heard a female voice calling out behind him. Abruptly, Martin turned around to see who it was.

She was rushing towards him.

As she got closer, Martin recognised her. She was the waitress at the restaurant where he just ate lunch. Her black velvet dress was shimmering in the sunshine.

"I'm sorry, miss..." Martin touched the brim of his hat and nodded at her. "Did I forget to pay for lunch or something?"

"No, of course you paid for it! But I didn't call you for that," the girl replied in a soft, gentle voice. She looked as gentle and sweet as her voice. Anyone who saw her would certainly take a second look at her pretty face.

"I think you forgot this." She handed Martin a piece of paper.

Martin took it, realising what it was, and glanced over it quickly... For a moment, he thought it might cause trouble, but when he saw her smile he realised he was mistaken.

"Don't worry," the girl reassured him. "I don't like to interfere in other people's business. That's why I came to return it to you." She looked at Martin with a wide, candid smile.

Although Martin was relieved, he did not say so. The truth was that he had left the piece of paper on the table on purpose, in the aim of getting the girl's attention. It was really only for a bit of fun.

He had half-expected her to be annoyed and when he had seen her coming to return the paper, he thought she might be coming to make a fuss. On the contrary, she appeared to want to get to know him and, although he was pleased, he couldn't help but wonder why.

"Thank you, miss!" Martin smiled back at her, "but may I know why you thought this trifling bit of paper so important?"

"I'm sorry Mr…"

"Martin, Martin Laslore."

"Yes, Mr. Martin. I don't think I've ever seen you in Greentown. I thought perhaps this was your first visit and that you didn't know the place. If that is the case, then I expect you'll be careful from now on."

Martin now understood.

She had come to threaten him, albeit in a very tactful way.

Did she always act this cool when she was

angry? Martin wondered. He had thought that the girl was being friendly towards him, but in fact it was completely the opposite.

Martin pulled himself together, "Of course, miss, I will definitely heed your warning," he said quickly.

"I'm glad to hear that." Then the girl turned away and walked back to the bar, swaying her head in annoyance.

Strange! Martin thought to himself as he waved her goodbye, *Well, we will meet again for sure!* Muttering these words he tore up the piece of paper and threw it to the winds. He had not written anything special on it, just a single line: *You can only be compared to yourself.*

Well, he supposed he had a bit of fun!

But the girl was obviously smart; she could make trouble if she wanted. Maybe she hadn't wanted to waste the opportunity to show off her personality and that was why she had not said much. The slightest move on her part would be enough; the entire town could show him the fun he was thinking about!

Damn! Martin slapped himself hard on the head. Such extravagance thoughts always puts him in danger.

Anyway, Martin watched the girl going into the bar, realising that he didn't even know her name. Then he continued on his way, rolling a cigarette and putting it between his lips.

The footpath was dusty and dirty. Now and then unpleasant smells assailed his nose and the dust blew continuously into his face.

He pressed his bandana against his nose.

He observed both sides of the road as he walked along. There were many buildings on either side, some big and some small - stables, a general store, a saloon, a café, a law office, a church… everything was there.

But at that precise moment, Martin was thinking about a clean room in a hotel.

He had been travelling for at least thirty-six

hours before he had at last discovered Greentown. First of all he had handed over his cherished black stallion to the stable hostler, and then he knew he too needed to rest. He thought he would take a shower and then have a good, sound sleep for three-four hours or so. That would be great!

Blowing out a cloud of smoke, Martin looked around him to find the signboard of a good hotel.

He stopped at a crossroads and decided to turn right. A little further on, he caught sight of a huge building.

The wooden walls were discoloured and not in very good condition, but above the batwing doors there hung a glittering signboard, highlighting the "Saliman Hotel & Saloon".

The place looked welcoming enough. Martin threw down his cigarette and crushed it under his boot.

There were a lot of people walking along the road, all occupied with their own affairs.

Nobody was interested in a stranger.

They didn't even notice him.

Martin realised it was not unusual for these people to have an unknown person in their midst.

He walked slowly towards the hotel. The hotel had a perfectly-shaped balcony and stairs leading up to the door.

All of a sudden a man burst through the door and almost collided with Martin. He looked slightly embarrassed as his hat fell off his head.

Martin moved aside to let him pass.

The man tried to pull himself together but was unable to do so, obviously because he had been drinking far too much.

Martin picked up the hat from the ground and handed it back to the man. He could see from the latter's ravaged face that he was seriously drunk.

"Hey man, pull yourself together!" Martin advised him, though feeling slightly repulsed.

"Damn!" the drunkard replied in an unsteady voice. "You can go now my friend!" Then he swung around as if nothing had happened and went on his way.

Martin went into the hotel.

There was a long counter with a shelf on the wall behind it where the keys were kept.

The bartender came forward to greet his new customer. He was a thin, black-skinned man with a pockmarked face.

"Howdy Mister! Welcome to the only best hotel in Greentown," the bartender welcomed him in a friendly voice.

"Thank you. I need a room," Martin said as he contemplated the saloon.

About ten people were sitting around, playing cards or drinking whisky and talking loudly to each other. Nobody looked at him.

"I have just one spare room at the moment, sir," the bartender told him, observing Martin's impressive physique.

"Has it got a shower?"

"Certainly, sir!"

The bartender selected a key from the numerous

bunches on the shelf behind him and handed it to him. He indicated the stairs with a smile. “Your room’s on the second floor. Number 14, sir.”

Martin took the key and paid the bartender, informing him that he would be resting until the evening. Then he started going upstairs. The bartender was surprised to see him that he had no baggage.

“Mr. Martin?” he called out as he checked his register. So, the man knew his name now. “Looks like you came here empty-handed?”

“That’s right, Saliman,” Martin confirmed, looking over his shoulder with a smile. Although he hadn’t introduced himself, he now realised that the bartender was also the proprietor.

“I’ll talk to you again this evening Saliman.”

Saliman smiled at the six-guns which were dangling from Martin’s waist.

He knew that they were not going to last long!

When the light started to fade from the sky, Martin went down. He had found it hard to get to sleep that afternoon, but fortunately there had been some books on the nightstand which he had skimmed through to pass the time before finally falling asleep. After his nap, he felt much fresher, both in body and mind.

Saliman’s bar was now very crowded and Martin

took a close look at everyone there. He saw that Saliman was busy at the counter taking orders and serving drinks.

Martin called a boy and asked him to fetch him a whisky. There was an old newspaper on the table, which he glanced carefully.

Martin put the newspaper back on the table. He remembered that he had to go out and buy a few necessities. Moreover, he had made up his mind to have supper at that pretty young woman's restaurant. He felt confident that he would get around her quite easily.

Martin found it hard to forget the way she had looked at him and her sweet, unfaltering smile.

He had never thought about a girl so seriously before.

But Martin knew that he could not get mixed up with any girl, unless he managed to lead a more stable life. Then maybe he could think about it. But for now, Martin had to stay away from her and to stop even thinking about her.

Martin swallowed the rest of the whisky in one go and stood up.

He wanted to find out more about the town from Saliman, but seeing the huge crowd in the bar he decided not to bother him just then and paid his bill to the boy. He informed the boy that he would not be there for supper then stepped out of the hotel.

Greentown might as well have been called Cattletown. Martin had followed the North trail to get there and had seen several ranches along the way, surrounded by grassland. The larger ranches must have had at least seven or eight hundred head of cattle and even the smaller ones must have had more than three hundred.

First of all, Martin went to the stables to check up on his stallion. He was satisfied with the service and gave the hostler boy a tip as he left. In return, the boy revealed some fresh news from town. It seemed that many unwanted strangers had recently turned up in Greentown and there had been a lot of fighting and shooting. There was no more law and order in the town. Just a couple of days ago there had been a bank robbery and, before that, eighty heads of cattle had been stolen from Garry's ranch.

The news pleased Martin for some reason!

Martin left the stables, found a tailor's shop and ordered some clothes and a pair of boots, saying he would call by and collect them on his way back to the hotel.

*

The tailor was the spitting image of a chimpanzee and appeared to be a depot of fat! He asked Martin if he had come to town on business or if he were perhaps looking for work. Martin didn't reply to these inquisitive questions and simply put his money on the table. But as he left the store, he heard the man advising him to be cautious, "You should be more careful, stranger. There are certain people in this town who don't care about having a good reason or excuse to cause trouble."

Martin walked away respecting the tailor's words. It was hard for him to hide his smile as he didn't expect such serious words from this strange looking guy!

He also wanted to go to the general store, but he was tired of walking, so he went straight to the restaurant. He didn't know why, but he felt as if the pretty girl was calling him!

Martin hurried along.

The restaurant's name was ***Jay and Jenny's Restaurant***, so he guessed her name was Jenny. Martin expected to see her when he went inside, but instead he saw a boy of about sixteen or seventeen, who was taking care of the bar. He looked very much like Jenny.

"Evening stranger! Welcome to *Jan's dug-out!*" Hearing his voice, Martin was sure that he must be Jenny's brother. But he could not see Jenny anywhere in the restaurant.

"Thanks Jan, I came to have some supper." Martin smiled. He put three dollars on the table and asked for the menu. "I want to eat until my stomach bursts!"

"Of course Mr…."

"It's Martin, Martin Laslore."

"Yes, Mr. Martin. You don't seem to be a hawker like a lot of the other strangers," Jan said in an indifferent voice. "Can I ask you something?"

"Well, yes of course." Martin was trying to find an excuse to ask him about Jenny's whereabouts, so that he would feel a little calmer.

"Are you staying in town for long?"

"That depends. My pistols will help me to decide." Martin gave a smile by pressing his lips.

"But I assume you have some money and I guess you haven't come here to look for work."

Martin thought Jan was a bright young fellow.

"You're right." Said Martin but quickly switched to his own interest for a sec just before he asked about Jenny, "If I need some money, then I must go to the bank. Though I heard about the robbery and bankruptcy… "

"In that case, you can go to another bank instead."

Martin realised that if he wanted to find out about Jenny from the boy - tactfully or not – he would be caught out. Jan seemed to consider him to be quite the gentleman.

Forget about that girl, you fool! Martin's own conscience remonstrated with him.

He sat at the table and ate his supper hungrily. Then he gave a satisfied burp.

A hot cup of tea came almost immediately.

As he sipped, he looked round him, sizing everyone up, but still he couldn't get Jenny out of his mind. He wondered where she could have gone. Did her family have a ranch? If they did, maybe she had finished work and gone home.

Suddenly Martin was startled by a thud as the door opened.

Four boys burst into the restaurant.

They were wearing flannel shirts and Ski trousers. Their hats were hanging from drawstrings on their backs.

They looked like trouble.

Martin was drinking his tea and trying to ignore them, but all of a sudden he heard a noise like a loud slap.

He looked at Jan.

Jan was trembling, either from fear or anger, and his hand had gone to his cheek. Two of the boys had gone behind the counter. One of them had grabbed Jan's collar and was shaking him vigorously. He seemed to be the leader of the gang and was the one who had slapped Jan.

"Jan, you dared fight with one of my men," the boy said angrily. "So you must pay for it now!"

"Your people stole some cattle from us!" Jan retorted as he managed to pull his collar from his grasp. Martin could clearly see the mark on his cheek where he had been slapped. "Not only that, Larry and Cat behaved wrong with my sister."

"I also want to say something to Jenny too! And if she agrees…"

"You've said enough, Vic!" Jan was bursting with rage now. He pointed a threatening finger at Vic. "Don't you dare say another dirty word about my sister."

"Or else you'll have to call me your brother-in-law, I suppose!" The guy called Vic laughed jeeringly and the rest of the gang followed suit.

Jan was on the verge of punching Vic in the face out of sheer rage, but the other boys caught hold of him to restrain him.

Jan struggled in vain to get free.

Then Vic slapped him on his other cheek.

Jan screamed in pain.

The other boys started to laugh sadistically at seeing him so helpless. Suddenly it was as if a thunderbolt had hit the restaurant!

First there was the sound of a gunshot and immediately afterwards the noise of something breaking on the floor!

The floor was wet and there were pieces of broken coffee mug.

For a moment or two it was so silent inside the restaurant that everyone could have heard a pin drop.

"What's wrong Mister?" Vic shouted at Martin.

Everybody was looking at Martin now, as if they hadn't noticed him until now.

Martin pushed his chair against the wall and put his legs on the table, sorting a more relaxed seating position.

He was smiling at them, as if in mockery, and twirling his pistol in his hand. There was smoke curling out of the barrel and disappearing into the air.

"My tea cup couldn't abide your nonsense, so it aimed right at your head," Martin explained in a matter-of-fact voice. "If the bullet from my pistol hadn't broken it, then maybe it would have broken your head, Vic!"

Vic shuffled uneasily and Martin fired his pistol again. Everybody was astonished to see Vic's pistol fall from his gun belt.

"Friends, just stay where you are and don't try to move again. And you two, I'd be glad if you would release Jan at once," Martin said in an ice-cold voice. "Jan, take those nasty things out of their holsters and hand them over to me."

Jan obeyed orders and the boys were too frightened to protest. Someone who could drop a pistol from its holster at twenty paces simply had to be respected. Nobody dared speak to him except for Vic, who frowned at Martin, "Hey Mister! Why are you nosing into our business?" he asked with disgust.

"Because, I don't like extra trouble around me

when I am in good mode," Martin replied. "But we're not finished here yet. Jan," he went on, looking at Jan, "you have the mark of ten fingers on your cheek; I want to see the same on Vic's!"

Jan was smiling now.

He understood that he need not be afraid as long as he had a person like Martin beside him, so he walked towards Vic confidently.

"You're overdoing it, stranger!" said Vic aggressively, looking angrily at Jan. But Jan completely ignored this remark and went up to him.

After a moment a loud slap echoed round the restaurant and Vic fell to the ground.

"Bravo Jan, bravo! But what about his other cheek?" Martin asked innocently, clapping with the hand that held his pistol and looking as if he were really enjoying the whole thing.

Jan tried to pull Vic up to his feet, but Vic pushed him away and stood up by himself. His lips were bleeding. He wiped the blood away. The other three boys were standing like dummies, not uttering a word.

"I can't help congratulating you on your courage, stranger," Vic said seriously. "But remember that I'll get my own back some other day."

Martin put his pistol back into its holster and rolled a cigarette, pretending not to hear him. Vic looked at Jan menacingly. "And you, Jan, be sure you'll be seeing me again. I'm leaving now, but I'll be back!"

One of Vic's followers shouted out, "give us back our guns!"

"I guess you haven't yet returned Jan's cattle. When you've done that, then you can get your toys back, kid!" said Martin, nonchalantly.

"Hey look…" Vic's voice rose again, but he was interrupted.

"Jan, tell these guys to get out of my sight. Otherwise, if my pistol comes out of its holster a second time, there'll be blood all over this place."

The boys were afraid to say another word and turned to leave. But they were looking at Martin as if to say, *"Alright, but we'll meet again!"* And it looks like Martin just catches these words!

"I hope to see you again, my friends!" Martin echoed their thoughts as he bade them goodbye.

He looked at Jan, who was gazing at him in admiration. Jan had discovered that this *"gentleman"* was not quite as he had imagined.

Suddenly they heard the sound of the door opening and Martin saw Jenny coming into the restaurant. She was almost running and looking very agitated, as if she had heard some terrible news.

"Are you alright Jan?" Jenny ran to Jan and threw her arms round her brother. "For God's sake…!" She was sobbing. Tears were running slowly down her silky cheeks.

CHAPTER 3

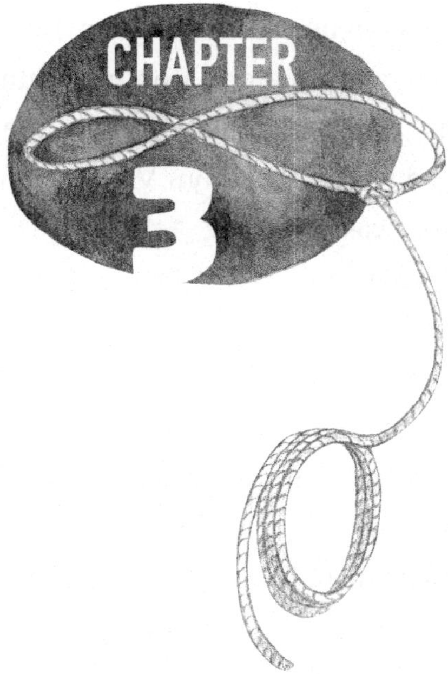

The sheriff was leaning against a pillar with his hands on his chest.

Although not really good-looking, he was a tall, well-built man whose demeanour gave off an air of self-assurance. His cool yet alert eyes clearly expressed that he was very cunning, the kind of man who, if necessary, would not hesitate to attack someone from behind.

The person he was waiting for came at last.

Jenny approached slowly, plunged in her thoughts. She was thinking about the person who had saved her brother from Vic.

Martin was his name.

His handsome, yet friendly face kept coming into Jenny's mind.

Who was this man?

And why had he come to Greentown?

Unless it was for business or work, hardly anybody ever came to this town. Those who came were often rustlers or other kinds of outlaws. But was there anybody as charming and nice-looking as Martin? Certainly not!

"I beg your pardon, miss," the sheriff interrupted her contemplation. "I need to talk to you about something." He removed his hat and bowed to her.

"What's the matter, sheriff?" Jenny acted as though she was really surprised to see him.

That girl can't give up her habit of interfering! The sheriff swore silently to himself. Then he gave her a forced smile and came to the point.

"Miss Jenny, I heard there was some trouble at your restaurant yesterday."

"I guess you must have dreamt that up!" Jenny

replied.

The sheriff ignored the remark. He was feeling rather embarrassed in her presence. He knew that if he wanted to talk to her directly then he could lose his job. So he pulled himself together and said, "Miss, you should beware of that new guy, Martin Laslore. You may not know, but…"

Jenny stopped him right there.

"I was just thinking about a way to replace you with him," she said, looking him straight in the eye.

"You can do that, miss, but…"

"Sheriff, I hope you know by now that I don't have any time to waste talking about such nonsense. You've told me what you had to tell me and I have listened. You may go now." Jenny said this lightly, though she realised that she was being a little insolent.

But the sheriff was not upset at all. Instead, he waited for Jenny to finish what she was saying.

"Please try to understand," he said solemnly. "I need to share some important information with you about this Martin guy."

Jenny did not reply straight away.

She saw that the sheriff was perfectly serious and she wondered what the matter was.

Why was he so concerned about Martin?

Was Martin actually a law-breaking vagabond?

Of course, it could also be possible that he was actually innocent but a convict in the eyes of law. You can never tell a person by his appearance or guess what is in his mind.

Jenny nodded at him and said, "Alright. Let's not waste any more time - tell me what you want to say."

"Not here, miss. Let's go to my office."

Jenny hesitated for a moment, but finally agreed to go with him.

The sheriff smiled at her indulgently.

He indicated that Jenny should walk in front of him and followed her to his office, which was not far away.

Martin looked out the window of his hotel room and saw that his lovely Jenny was talking to a man. The man looked as though he was eager to impart something, but Jenny was not paying much attention.

Who was this man and what did he want from Jenny?

Why did the man seem familiar to him?

Ah, now he remembered - he was that drunk guy who had collided with him yesterday outside Saliman's hotel. But what did this drunkard want from Jenny? Though at present, nobody could really label him as a drunk; he was quite the gentleman.

It's disgusting! Whatever am I thinking about? Martin murmured to himself.

After all, Jenny was a respectable girl and the townspeople admire her. Anybody had the right to talk to her if they wanted to.

Martin watched Jenny accompanying the man to the other side of the footpath and going into a lane on the right. She seemed to be asking the man something and they gradually disappeared from view.

Martin moved away from the window, repressing his thoughts.

There was a small mirror on one of the wooden walls in his room and he scrutinised his face closely.

For several days he had not been able to shave and he was beginning to get a rough beard, which made him look older than his age. He looked about thirty when, in reality, he had only just turned twenty five. The advantage was that his newly grown beard and moustache hid his face and made it difficult to recognise him. Martin preferred it that way since he didn't want people to show too much interest in him. Until now, anyone who had shown excessive curiosity had not been allowed to live.

Thinking about the past, a wicked smile spread across his face.

He looked over his shoulder and glanced at his money belt that was lying on the bed. It contained exactly five thousand dollars. For now he could put the money in a bank and start doing his job. As far as he could judge, the inhabitants of Greentown weren't interested in interfering in other people's business. If that were true, then he could think about getting a small ranch nearby. However, he knew that to do that, it would be impossible to avoid the influential people in the town and then there would probably be problems with lawsuits. Then again, it might not be so much of a problem if he could strike up a friendship with them. There had been certain problems in his past, however, which, if he could not clear them up, would prevent him from going ahead with his plans. It seemed that the right time had not yet come to deal with the mess. Maybe it would sort itself out when the right time came, or maybe someone else could sort it for him. The main thing was that if everything went according to plan, then Martin could manage the rest of it easily. He would not need anybody else…

There was a loud knock on his door, which jolted Martin back to reality. He heard Saliman's voice outside and opened the door. Saliman was standing in the corridor with a smile on his face. He was a very thin man and so tall that he would probably have to bend a little to enter the room. But Saliman did not go in. He stood at the door and said, "Good morning sir, I hope you slept well."

"Very well, thank you. Your hotel is really nice. I'm very satisfied." Martin said, leaning on the door frame.

"Thank you very much, sir." Saliman's smile spread even wider. "Sir, Mr. Robertson is here to see you. He's waiting for you downstairs."

"Robertson?"

"He's the foreman at the *Triple J* ranch. Perhaps Mr. Jerri sent him."

"Are you talking about the owner of *Jay and Jenny's Restaurant*?"

"Yes indeed, sir!"

"Alright, tell him to wait a minute. I'll come downstairs." Martin closed the door, leaving Saliman still standing there.

He went to the bed quite calmly and took off his shirt. His muscly, hairy chest, and wide shoulders displayed unusual strength.

He took the money belt from the bed and strapped it onto his shoulder. Then he put on one of the new flannel shirts that he had bought from the tailor's shop the day before and tidied himself up. At last he emerged from his room with his gun belt hanging from his waist.

He was wondering for what reason Mr. Jerri might have sent for him. He thought that the only plausible answer was that he wanted to thank him for saving his only son. Perhaps he wanted to warn him about Vic as well. Yes, it would be alright if that was the case - but if the man suddenly asked him about something else? As a rule, Martin could not bear excessive interest in him, but for something like this he supposed it would be alright. It was normal to show a little interest in a new face.

Martin went slowly downstairs. He saw a short, stout man with a plump face standing in front of the counter. He was wearing cowboy clothes, with a hat on his bald head. He must have been forty or fifty years old.

The man heard the sound of footsteps and turned towards the stairs. He smiled at Martin and welcomed him warmly.

"Hello Mister, you must be Martin?"

Martin smiled too and held out his hand.

"You recognised me right away, Mr. Robertson."

Robertson shook his hand and looked at him reproachfully.

"Nope!" he exclaimed, "You must call me Robert." Then he looked at Martin from head to toe, as if to make a thorough examination. He raised his eyebrows. "Hm! Jan didn't lie to me - you really are a handsome man!"

"Thank you," Martin replied, unembarrassed by the praise. He knew that people like Robert were usually very friendly and genuine. They were the kind of people he appreciated.

Also, they did not generally create trouble intentionally, although they didn't usually spare troublesome people either.

They left the hotel together. Robert's horse was hitched to a rail. Martin saw that his stallion was standing beside it, as he had requested to the hostler boy earlier. The men mounted their horses and moved off slowly.

They had not gone very far when they heard a loud cry and saw smoke rising up above the stores on the east side of the town.

They spurred their horses and galloped towards the smoke to find out what had happened.

As they got closer to the scene, they could hear people screaming in fright. It was clear that there had been an outbreak of fire and everybody was rushing about trying to extinguish it.

CHAPTER 4

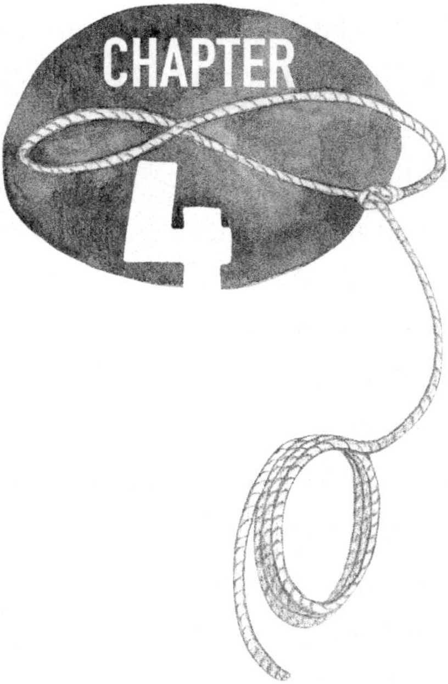

A man entered the sheriff's office, completely out of breath.

He looked as if he were being chased by a ghost and had to run as fast as his legs could carry him to get there! He was panting heavily and could hardly speak. When he saw that Jenny was talking to the sheriff, he lost his nerve and seemed unsure about what should be done in such a situation. But the sheriff rescued him from this awkwardness.

"What is it?" the sheriff asked, realising that it was something important. At any other time, he would have bawled the man out for surging into his office without permission.

The man pulled himself together and wiped the sweat off his forehead.

"Sheriff, Navice's newspaper stand has been burned to the ground! I heard that it was done intentionally!"

"What?!" The sheriff leaped out of his chair.

"Yes, poor Navice is in despair."

"What's that you say? Let's go there quickly!" The sheriff picked up his hat from the desk and addressed Jenny.

"Sorry miss, I have to go. But, think about what I said. I'll see you later."

With that, he hurried from the office. Jenny stood up to leave as well. The bringer of bad tidings nodded at her. Then he turned and rushed back out of the office.

When the sheriff arrived on the scene, the onlookers had calmed down. There were only a few people talking with lowered voices.

He looked at Navice's stand, without

dismounting his horse. The stand had completely collapsed and nothing remained of it except a heap of black ashes. The smoke was still blowing in the wind.

Two of the adjacent stores had also been affected by the flames, but had fortunately not suffered too much damage.

The sheriff looked at the crowd of people and got off his horse and walked towards them.

When they saw the sheriff coming, the disgruntled mumbling turned into inaudible whispering.

The sheriff spotted Robertson, the foreman of the *Triple J* ranch. Robertson was standing there looking annoyed, with Martin at his side.

"Sheriff!" Robertson called out rather resentfully, "please can you do something about these stupid people!"

"What's going on here?" the sheriff inquired.

"They're all claiming that I'm the one who set fire to Mr. Navice's store…" Martin answered, although he did not seem over-worried.

"…which is not possible," Robertson added, "since I brought Mr. Martin here just now from the hotel."

"No, that's a lie!" someone shouted from the crowd.

"It was him! He set fire to the store!" someone else chimed in.

Again there was a hullabaloo, but the sheriff put his hands up and protested with a roar, "are you going to stop that?!... Where is Navice?"

A man appeared from the midst of the crowd. He was short with bloodshot eyes from continuous crying.

"May I know what you have to say?" the sheriff asked him.

"Yes, Sheriff, this man set fire to my store!" Navice pointed his finger at Martin, but the latter did not react. He was standing very still and erect.

"How do you know? Was he next to you when it happened?"

"No, he was running away after setting the stand on fire – I saw him then."

He took a hat from another person's hand and showed it to the sheriff. "When he was running away, this hat fell off his head."

The sheriff took the hat. Martin was surprised to see that it really was his hat and that he wasn't wearing a hat now.

Then he remembered that the night before he had heard some strange noises in his room. Now it occurred to him that a thief must have stolen the hat and that the thief must be very cunning…

Was it Vic?!

"Does this hat belong to you, Mr. Martin?" the sheriff asked him.

"Yes…" Martin hesitated a moment. "But I have no idea how it got here!"

"Because you came here with it!" Navice suggested angrily.

"Did you see my face?"

"Of course… I still remember your devilish smile."

"Don't talk silly, Navice! Think again, who did you see exactly?" the sheriff asked impatiently.

"I repeat that it was definitely this man."

"So…" the sheriff looked at Martin helplessly. "You must understand, stranger, that you have to come with me…"

"This can't be happening Sheriff!" Robertson protested. "You can talk to Saliman if you want."

"Everything will be done according to the proper procedure, Robert, but first things first…"

There was a loud cry among the people: "We

need compensation!"

"Look, Sheriff, I agree to give compensation, if that will make things any better," Martin declared, "but I assure you I'm innocent."

The sheriff shrugged his shoulders.

"I'm helpless here. You must come with me. It's my official duty."

Martin didn't insist. He knew there was no point in saying anything more, though he was not really worried. He knew that only Vic would do something so stupid.

"Don't worry Mr. Martin, I am..." Robertson was trying to say something, but Martin stopped him with a smile. "Don't worry about me, there won't be any problem!" Then he looked at the crowd and caught sight of Vic's malevolent face and saw that his companions were with him as well.

There was a malicious smile on their faces! But Martin only winked at them and smiled.

Miss, Martin Laslore is a bounty hunter...

The words were echoing in Jenny's brain. This was what the sheriff had told her before she left his office.

A bounty hunter in Greentown!

That meant there was a possibility of huge chaos in the town. Bounty hunters did not wander around for no reason. Their job was to shoot notorious outlaws or fugitives and demand rewards in return. If Martin were a bounty hunter, then who was he looking for?

Jenny pondered for a while.

She didn't recall seeing any strangers in the town lately who looked suspicious or liable to be wanted. Moreover, all the people who carried out illegal actions had no fear of any legal steps being taken against them. Everybody did what they wanted to do in public. So there must be a reason behind Martin Laslore's arrival here.

Of course Jenny had not believed the sheriff at first. But when he put the wanted list in front of her eyes and said, *"I picked up this paper outside Saliman's hotel yesterday, disguised as a drunk..."* she looked and saw Martin's picture. There was no reason to distrust the sheriff now.

No, it must be true. Martin Laslore must indeed be a bounty hunter.

If Jenny had been an ordinary girl, the sheriff would not even have bothered to warn her about Martin. Jenny knew this very well and she knew the reason behind it too. But she was not worried about that.

She had left the office almost immediately after the sheriff. She went to the restaurant and directly to the kitchen. When her father, Mr. Jerri, learned that Martin was a bounty hunter, he would have only one idea in his head and that would be to chase Martin away. He had been having trouble with the ranch lately and if there were more trouble on top of that, then it would become hard to stay in Greentown.

But why am I thinking about all this? Jenny scolded herself.

She washed her hands in the basin and dried them with the towel that was hanging in front of the mirror.

Suddenly she saw a person behind her in the mirror.

She sprang around at once.

"Johnson!" Jenny exclaimed happily. She looked appraisingly at the young man standing before her.

"You were supposed to stay in Glitter City today…" she started.

"Uh huh… I was supposed to be in the afterlife instead of Glitter City, and it's very lucky that I am standing in front of you now!" the young man joked.

"Don't say such things! Tell me what the matter is really," Jenny insisted.

"I've told you the truth, Jenny! I went to Glitter alright, but the Borhan's outlaws attacked us on the way. If that stranger hadn't turned up, maybe I would be…"

Jenny stopped him by pressing her finger to his lips. She went nearer to him.

"Don't talk like that! It makes me sick."

Johnson smiled at her and made as if to embrace her. But Jenny stood aside quickly.

"So tell me, what happened exactly?"

"We camped at Glossy Mountain and were resting by the fire. Suddenly, out of the blue, bullets started raining down on us and we were so startled that we didn't have the time to defend ourselves. There was a horseman near the trail and he came to help us. Honestly, if it hadn't been for him we wouldn't be alive right now. The belongings were unharmed, but Dowdy was slightly injured."

"It's a relief that nothing much was damaged," Jenny agreed. She sighed. "Did the man go with you?"

"No, I went on to Glitter. He asked me if there was any town nearer, so I told him about Greentown, so he must have arrived before us. Do you know who came to town recently?"

"A man called Martin," Jenny replied. There was sweat on her forehead from anxiety.

"Oh yes! That was the name the man gave us. Good, I'll find an opportunity to thank him!"

"But before that, tell me if you've had your breakfast or not," Jenny said, changing the subject. Johnson frowned and put his hand on his stomach.

"How can you imagine that I'd have breakfast anywhere other than at your place?!"

He caught hold of Jenny from behind and put his arms around her. Jenny tried to wriggle free. At last Johnson gave up and they both burst out laughing.

Jenny gave him a big hug, smiling and blushing.

Johnson was the son of Robertson, the foreman. She wasn't sure about his feelings, but she knew quite well that he was the only man she could ever love.

When she dreamed about the future, she knew he was the only man she could trust…

CHAPTER 5

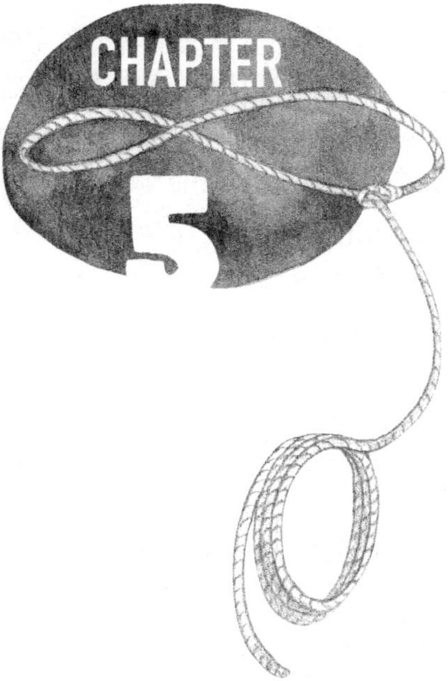

Martin did not have to stay long at the sheriff's office. With Robertson's help, he soon obtained his release. Even so, he still had to pay for his bail. As he left the office, Martin noticed that a stranger, leaning on a pillar, was looking straight at him. The man then quickly merged into the crowd. Martin and Robertson mounted their horses and headed towards the *Triple J* ranch.

They were cantering along the rough trails when Robertson asked Martin, “Mr. Martin, may I know where you were the day before yesterday? I mean where did you come from?”

Martin smiled at him.

“I was in a town called Glitter City,” he replied, “where I stayed for a couple of days before coming here directly.”

Robertson looked at him with a hint of curiosity on his face.

“Glitter City! Strange!! Now, I hope you won’t deny that you also stopped at Glossy Mountain and that you saved a wagon along with a bunch of people from a group of ambushers? ”

“And over chief Johnson is one of your people. I heard the name of this town from him. Otherwise, I would probably be roaming aimlessly towards South Capasi by now. That young man told me that he was going to Glitter City on behalf of *Triple J* ranch. By the way, has he returned?”

“Yes, he returned this morning. As a matter of fact, he’s my son. He told me all about it.”

“What more did you hear?” Martin asked him with acute interest. Suddenly he felt a little numb.

“I didn’t ask him anything else,” Robertson

replied, “but, I imagine that Jerri has already made his investigations about you. When strangers arrive in the town, he’s got into the habit of finding out as much as he can about them. He lost a lot of money in the bankruptcy a couple of days ago. We assume it was an inside job and that some of his employees may also have helped the rustlers steal the cattle. These incidents only take place when some new guys come to town and they disappear almost immediately. Because of this, Jerri has decided to keep an eye on all strangers. But…”

“But I hope you don’t think that about me?” Martin interrupted him. “You can be sure that Mr. Jerri will introduce me to you in a completely different way.”

He smiled at Robertson as if he were joking.

Martin felt relieved when he heard nothing that he might have expected.

He was more comfortable now.

The foreman did not ask him anything further and he shrugged his shoulders. After a while he resumed the conversation but on a different subject.

“I think that Vic wanted to send you to jail!”

“Why do you say that?”

“You’ve just arrived in town so you’re not

acquainted with the people here. I'm convinced that Old Nick bribed Navice in order to send you to jail."

"Hmm... and that's why I don't want to waste my time by charging Navice!" Martin nodded.

"But remember, if you don't pay him back then he won't let you sleep in peace. He doesn't have the guts to pull the trigger, but he sure knows how to annoy someone."

"I don't have any problem with that, in fact I'd rather enjoy it. As long as I'm here, I can play with that brat - I'll consider it as a kind of exercise."

"Well said!" Robertson approved, pulling the reins to slow down.

Martin looked around him. A little further along the trail, on the right, there was a small lake among the meadows. On either side of the lake there were ornamental gardens and, right beside it, a huge ranch enclosed by fences.

Beyond the ranch, the surroundings were magnificent, as if painted in water colours. Cattle were grazing in the pastures and on the north side of the ranch there was a big forest of cottonwood trees.

"We're here, this is our ranch," the foreman

announced as got out of his saddle.

Martin hitched his horse and followed the foreman quietly. There were bushes and plants in the fields that Martin could not name, as well as a lot of eucalyptus trees scattered here and there.

Martin followed Robertson through the gate. A narrow, concrete path crossed the garden and led to the ranch's store.

A thin, unhealthy-looking cowboy took their horses. More than five cowboys were in the stables, busy at work. There was a small shack nearby where it was apparent that the cooking was done; appetising fumes were rising up into the air. In spite of the mess, the worker's environment seemed quite comfortable.

The cooking shack, bunkhouse and various sheds were situated on each side of the narrow path.

There was a farm on the bank of the lake. The water in the lake glimmered in the sunshine.

Martin and Roberson went to the balcony on the outer part of the ranch house.

Almost immediately a man emerged from inside. His figure and build were exactly like Robertson's, and apart from his clothes, which were elegant and refined, he could easily be mistaken for Robertson's twin brother. His skin was sunburnt and he had fair hair and a moustache.

It was clear from his imposing bearing that this was Jerri, the owner of the ranch.

He frowned when he saw Martin beside Robertson. His face looked a bit like Jenny's and his eyes were the same shape and colour as Jan's.

"A new guest in our town, Jerri!" Robertson gestured towards Martin. "But your face is telling me something else."

"You two sit down," Jerri indicated a bench, and sat in a chair himself. He examined Martin from head to toe.

"Why are you so late, Robert?" inquired Jerri.

"There was a bit of trouble in town," Robertson explained as he hung his hat on a hook on the wall. "You know! But tell me what the matter is."

"I'll tell you… Howdy Mr. Martin. Nice to meet you in person."

The rancher smiled at Martin. Martin nodded back at him respectfully. He thought that the man had sent for him out of courtesy, but the conversation soon proved to the contrary.

Martin, who had remained standing, now sat down on the bench. He felt quite safe in this place.

"First let me express my utmost gratitude, Mr. Martin, for saving the restaurant and preventing Jan from fighting with Vic. You also saved Johnson from great danger…" Jerri pulled something out of his pocket.

"I am only doing my job, Mr. Jerri. I am…"

"Son, I think I understand what you're saying," Jerri interrupted him, "but the matter is slightly different. You've come from the West, so maybe you grew up in rough territory and that's why you take more time to understand the situation and how to work things out." As he said this, Jerri handed some papers to Robertson. Robertson looked at the papers attentively, his bald head shining as he bent forward.

"What are you trying to say, Mr. Jerri?"

Martin really did not understand what the rancher was trying to get at, but now he was beginning to suspect something fishy.

"Think hard, Mr. Martin. Immediately after you got to town you had a bit of trouble. Then there were some other unexpected problems you had to avoid. But although you might not believe it, the town wasn't like this just a couple of months ago. The townspeople and the ranchers – we all lived here peacefully. Everything was in order. But now we keep experiencing crimes. Suddenly there are more cow thieves than ever. Bank looting has increased and new strangers are coming into town too often. I don't know who is behind all this, but it seems like some opportunists want to turn this town into their own territory. At least that's what it looks like."

Martin shifted rather uncomfortably on the bench. He guessed that his true identity was no longer a secret. For some reason, the rancher was trying to tell him that he was well aware of Martin's purpose for coming to town.

As Robertson lifted his head up from the papers, Martin looked at them both squarely in the eye.

"I hope you're not taking me for the kind of person who is responsible for corrupting your town?"

"Son, it doesn't suit you to act stupid! But maybe you didn't get the meaning of my words? So, I'd better tell you directly."

The rancher looked at Robertson, "What do you say Robert?"

"That would be best," Robertson agreed. "At least that's what I think after reading these."

Robertson indicated the papers that he was still holding. The rancher took them and gave them to Martin.

"Mr. Martin, take a look at these and you'll understand what I'm trying to say."

Martin had been right in his suspicions. Perhaps it was Johnson who had collected this information from Glitter City. If not, the leaflets must have arrived in town along with the newspapers. If that were the case, then there was no point in hiding his identity any longer.

"Mr. Jerri, now I understand. You think I'm a bounty hunter and that I must have come to Greentown in pursuit of some notorious criminal. If that were true, then there would indeed be a risk of disaster. You think that if there is any trouble because of me, then your town will be destroyed."

"That's right. If that happens, then things will be out of our hands, out of the ranchers' hands. So to save this town…" Mr. Jerri stopped as Martin stood up again.

"You are advising me to leave town, aren't you? But do you think..." Martin indicated the money belt suspended from his shoulders, "that I am still carrying out my past profession?"

"What do you mean?" The rancher looked puzzled.

"You should enquire more about me, I am worse than a vagabond right now. Yes, it's true that I was in that profession a couple of days ago, but all the money I've collected has made me dream of other things. So, I've given up being a bounty hunter. I hope that's clear to you?" Martin smiled at them.

"Bad boy!" Robertson exclaimed.

"Does this mean that you've decided to stay in town?"

"Of course! And I propose that you help me get a job. In return, I can assure you that there won't be any trouble in town because I shall be there to prevent it." Mr. Jerri and Robertson looked at each other. Then Martin bade the "twins" goodbye. He went to the stables to fetch his horse and thanked the cowboy. Just then he saw a woman at the window, who he guessed must be Jenny's mother.

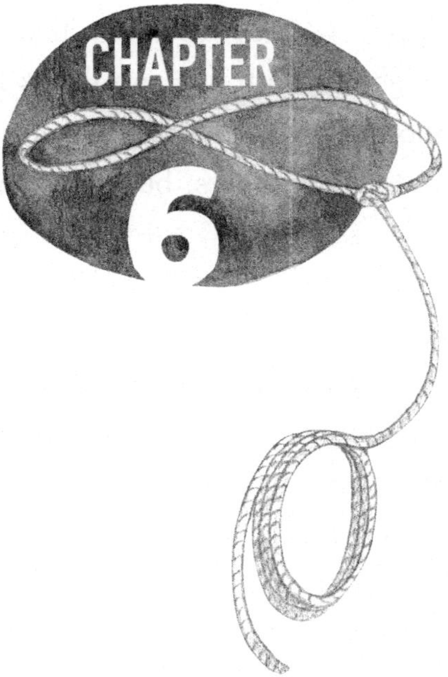

The second cow-hand, Johnson Hurt, the son of *Triple J* ranch's foreman Robertson Hurt, was not what one would call good-looking in a classical way, but there was something attractive about his appearance and physique which made people look at him twice. He was above average height, standing at about six feet tall, which caused the other young men in the town to show him a certain respect. They all knew that Johnson was more dangerous with his bare hands than when he was armed. Like his father, he was usually well-disposed towards others, but if he got angry, then beware!

Johnson never wore a holster unless it was absolutely necessary. He could cope easily with five men just with his bare hands, which was why the other young men usually kept their distance. However, Johnson was never unjust towards others.

In the case of Vic Rust, though, things were quite the opposite.

Vic was the son of Mathew Rust, the most influential rancher in the neighbourhood.

Johnson could not stand Vic and he knew very well that he was likely to lose control when Vic was near him.

Vic was aware of this too and for the sake of his own protection he usually avoided Johnson.

The basic rule of Greentown was that personal fights were to be carried out privately, which meant that Vic and his companions did not have the courage to go against Johnson. So Vic continued his crimes as sneakily as possible.

Johnson was rather surprised about Vic. It was

presumed that the latter's two companions had been involved in the theft of eighty head of cattle from the *Triple J* ranch a few days before.

That very day, the boys in question were on the way to Glitter City with five or six of their branded cows when Jan caught them red-handed. It was of course possible that they had stolen just a few cows to get some money for gambling and were using the fact that there had been an outbreak of rustling to dissimulate their own theft. But if things went on like this, after a while employees would be stealing cattle from their own ranches to make themselves more money.

Johnson was worried.

He could see the huge difference between the Greentown of the past and Greentown now. As the days went by, the heretofore carefree life of the townspeople was changing radically. Just a couple of months ago there would have been no need to carry a gun, but now people are obliged to take firearms to ensure their safety.

Why did this happen?

What was the problem?

What was the source of this problem?

In the last two months, about two and half

thousand head of cattle had been stolen from various ranches. The bank had been looted twice, causing some people to end up penniless. Nothing had been able to bring things under control and the thieves were continuing with their crimes.

The sheriff had done all he could to catch them, but to no avail. There was no sign of the bandits or even of their tracks. They succeeded in carrying out their robberies and then escaping without anyone seeing them.

It remained a mystery how the thieves could get away with stealing so many cattle!

The townsfolk couldn't understand it.

It was simply not possible that it was Borhan or some other gang. There must be some powerful outfit behind all this, who were hiding in Western Comanche or going through the counties with unbelievable skill. If this were the case, they would be able to disappear quite easily with the stolen cattle. But who were they? Who was responsible for this disaster? Who had hatched the plan to ruin this peaceful town after all these years?

Anyone influential in the town could be involved, which was an unsettling notion, but it was evident that someone from outside was pulling the strings. The person who had the ability and power to affect a nice quiet town within such a short time must be someone powerful.

Johnson didn't want to think about it; he could not imagine the fate of Greentown. He had left the restaurant, also perturbed by what he had heard there. Someone had informed him that a stranger called Martin had set fire to Navice's newspaper stand.

Martin!

It was a damned lie!

It must be Vic.

He heard that Vic had got into a fight with Martin at the restaurant the day before, which meant that Vic must be wild to take his revenge!

He thought the sheriff would send him to jail. But Johnson knew that his father had taken Martin to the ranch and that there would be no problem for Martin if he stayed with him.

It was nevertheless a disaster that Navice's stand had been burnt down. All the newspapers from Glitter must be burnt to ashes!

That week, the townspeople would not be able to read the news. It was Johnson's responsibility to bring the bundles of newspapers from Glitter City every week, since there was no private newspaper in Greentown.

Navice could not be blamed either – if he had started the fire himself, he must have done it because he was frightened of Vic. However, if he got compensation from the municipality as well as some money from Vic's bribe, then he would not have wasted his time!

Vic must be the one who was responsible for all this. He had gone too far this time and needed to be punished. It might be a good idea to put him out of action for a couple of days. It was for this reason that Johnson was heading towards Parcy's bar to look for Vic. He knew that at this time of the day Vic usually spent his time at that establishment.

Johnson had listened attentively to Jan's account of how Martin had succeeded in taking away the firearms from Vic and his companions. The guns had been handed over to the sheriff, although they would soon be returned to their owners. But he need not worry, Vic would never have the courage to shoot him even if he wasn't wearing a gun belt, because there was no way out if he shot Johnson.

Johnson was walking quickly along the footpath. His horse was hitched to the rail outside the restaurant.

As he walked, an idea came into Johnson's head about Martin. As far as he knew, the latter was a bounty hunter. He had stayed at Glitter for two nights. But where had he been before that? Since he was travelling around from one town to another, apparently at random, might he not be pursuing a criminal? If that were true, this would explain his arrival in Greentown. And if the criminal in question were really staying in the town, there was a fair chance that Martin would find him. If he did, and it was this criminal that was creating all the trouble in the town, then a lot could be gathered from questioning him. This was Johnson's assumption, but it would have to be verified.

Johnson stopped in front of Parcy's bar.

There were no familiar faces around. He went into the restaurant without hesitation.

About ten people were sitting around the tables inside. Most of them had just come in to get the latest gossip.

Johnson looked around him. He saw a complete stranger playing cards with Vic at the table in the corner.

Another man stood beside the stranger. He was

short, but looked as if he were as strong as the other one. They wore identical black hats with sparkling chains dangling from them. Vic was also with one of his companions. Johnson could tell from Vic's annoyed face that he was not good enough at the card game they were playing and was evidently losing.

Johnson went up to the counter and the bartender came to serve him, looking rather surprised. Johnson smiled at the astonishment on his face.

"Don't be surprised, Parcy. I've just come to give one of your customers here a lesson!"

Parcy threw a glance at Vic's table.

He was an elderly man, but still quite upright for his age. His hair, eye-brows, and large moustache were all as white as snow and his face was creased in wrinkles. He was still able to do his job, old Parcy, but it was understandable that he didn't want any trouble in his bar.

"OK," Parcy said, "but I'd rather you spared me that here."

"I think you should call the sheriff," Johnson went on, noticing that Vic had suddenly risen from his seat.

"Cheat! You deceived me!" Vic roared at the stranger, banging loudly on the table.

"Perhaps I should take your advice…." Johnson heard Parcy saying, without taking his eyes off Vic's table. Everybody in the saloon was now staring at Vic because of his sudden change of behaviour. "Give me back all my money Mister!" Vic shouted at the stranger who remained seated.

"I'm sorry, buddy." The stranger now stood up too, looking Vic straight in the eye. "I've earned that money playing honestly."

Some of the customers started leaving the saloon, assuming there would be a fight. The rest of them stood around eagerly, waiting to see what would happen. The two strangers looked at everyone in the saloon.

"You have insulted us, Mister," one of them said. "We have no time for this kind of behaviour. We must go." Saying this, the two strangers turned to leave.

Vic blocked their path. A couple of his friends joined him.

"Look Mister," the first stranger said, no longer smiling, "you should know how to behave better with gentlemen."

"Gentlemen!" Vic exclaimed with a smirk on his face.

"What do you say, Vic, that we take off these 'gentlemen's' clothes?" one of Vic's companions suggested.

"He…" Another one was about to make an equally stupid remark when a pistol shot rang out.

For a moment there was a deathly silence in the saloon. Then all of a sudden one of Vic's companions crumpled and fell to the floor with a hole in his head!

One of the strangers had a six-gun. The smoke was still curling out of its barrel.

Vic's gang was rooted to the spot from shock. In fact, everybody in the saloon was completely stunned.

This was the first murder in the history of Greentown!

Everybody needed some time to digest the incident.

"Stay where you are, don't move!" the first stranger ordered, brandishing his pistol. "When we've gone, you can dance if you like. But first, let me have your guns - ALL OF YOU!"

Everyone obediently placed their guns on the

table.

The stranger nodded to his companion, who methodically emptied the magazines of the pistols one by one. Then they both made towards the door, the man with the gun still treating the assembled company with his weapon.

Johnson was surprised to see that the two men could get away so easily after murdering someone. On the other hand, what could anyone do without a gun? Still, he was looking for an opportunity.

As the strangers passed in front of Johnson and moved cautiously towards the door, Johnson clenched his fists.

“If anyone tries to get to the door, they’ll get a bullet through the head!”

“Friends, I will try to send some tablets right through the heads, whom I will see first from the gate!” The second stranger threatened with a shotgun. Johnson wondered how he had managed to hide it under his coat!

The two strangers had almost reached the door when someone suddenly jumped out from behind it and kicked one of them violently in the chest.

As they were completely unprepared for such an attack, the one who had been kicked fell over on top of the other one. The latter lunged towards Johnson as he lost his balance.

Johnson was ready.

He struck the man's hand that was holding the shotgun. The stranger screamed out in pain and had no alternative but to drop the gun. Johnson punched him in the face, causing him to sprawl across one of the tables.

Just at that moment Johnson heard another gunshot.

He recognised the sheriff at once.

The sheriff's bullet had gone right through the other man's palm, obliging him to let go of the six-gun. He tried to pick it up again, but the sheriff kicked him hard on the forehead. His body flew through the air for a second or two before crashing down on the bar counter with a huge thud.

The man who had been kicked by Johnson now saw his advantage.

He had picked up his gun and was pointing it at Johnson, ready to pull the trigger, when a bullet hit him in the throat. Before there was time to react, the other stranger was shot with a bullet which flattened him against the counter.

The sheriff was astonished!

He looked at his pistol, which was still in his hand. Then he saw that Johnson was staring at something, so he looked too.

Everybody watched with wonder that a person was looking at everyone with a rather curious face. It was evident that he was the one who shot twice; the two pistols in his hands still had bluish smoke twirling from them.

Who else could it be but Martin – Martin Laslore!

About five hours later, four men were gathered in a small cabin. It was dark and rather creepy in the cabin. There was only one window, which was closed. In the corner, a rough-looking man was sitting on a chair. Two other men were standing beside him, leaning on the wall.

Their faces were cruel.

A man was walking up and down impatiently in

front of them.

This was Sheriff Dalton.

He was looking anxiously at the man who sat on the chair. But the latter ignored his gaze – he was staring at the floor, thinking about something else.

The other two men were standing like statues, as if they were waiting for something to happen.

They were dangerous people.

"So you're saying that you're not involved in these incidents? Then who is, huh?" The sheriff broke the silence in the room. "All this time has gone by without anyone ever being killed, not even a fly, and then in a couple of hours not one but three people are murdered!"

"Try to understand, sheriff," the man on the chair said in a cool voice. "No matter who is behind all these incidents in the town, they definitely have reasons other than rustling or bank robbery. They want to bankrupt the influential people and force them to leave, so that they can take over the town. Do you get what I mean?"

"There's logic in what you say, Borhan, but I want to know who it is! You're the only person to have come from another place. And anyhow, who attacked Johnson that night in the hills?"

"I know the townspeople will suspect me first. But you at least know me well enough, Sheriff. I was an outlaw, I don't deny it, but I have come to your town to make my life better. The people aren't letting me do this. They think that they shouldn't take the risk of sheltering an outsider. But you have given me that opportunity, Sheriff. After that, how could you imagine that I would betray your trust?"

"I'm not suspecting you, Borhan. But as a dangerous outlaw in the past, you can perhaps guess the plans of other rough-necked guys. I want to know who is responsible for these acts!"

"Whoever it is, he must be very cunning. In my opinion, he's working in a group. But my people are keeping an eye on any strangers to the town. You can ask Dave – he has already marked some of them." Borhan indicated one of his companions beside him.

Dave had a hair-bun and a French-cut beard.

"Sheriff, one of the people I'm suspecting is Mathew Rust's foreman," he said. "I've seen some strangers around his place."

Reeve, Borhan's bodyguard, who was standing on the left, added, "but the person who is at the top of our special list… Well, we won't say anything about him right now, sheriff, because we need to keep tabs on him for a couple of days more."

"So you can relax," Borhan added, stretching his arms and standing up. "We'll help you in every way we can."

"Thank you. But did you recognise the two guys who were killed?"

"Those two have been meeting Carl, Mathew's foreman," Dave replied.

"What!" the sheriff shouted. "In that case we should make some investigations about Carl immediately!"

"You can try, sheriff. But one thing - no matter how good a person Mathew Rust appears to be, keep him on your list." Borhan smiled.

"You're quite right. I've already put his son, Vic, behind bars. He'll be there for a couple of days, I guess. He's a brat. It was because of him that one of his companions was killed.

"Oh yes, by the way, why did you spare that Martin guy?"

"Well, if it hadn't been for him, we would have been dead by now."

"That guy knows me well and I know him too. There's nothing wrong with him."

"He's a bounty hunter."

"Yes he was, but now for the sake of his livelihood …. I heard he's planning to stay here?"

"Yes, I think so," the sheriff answered. "At first I thought he was a troublemaker, but now I think differently."

Suddenly there was a brief knock and all eyes turned to the door. One of the sheriff's men came into the cabin.

The sheriff shook hands with Borhan and made to leave the room. As he reached the door, he turned round again.

"Will you be leaving tonight?" he asked.

"No, I'll be staying at Saliman's hotel," Borhan replied.

When the sheriff had left, he looked at his companions with a smile on his face.

"We don't have to inform him for now that we've already spotted the real criminal," he said. "You must all work to get sufficient evidence. Then…" Borhan added.

Outside, the sheriff was feeling more relaxed.

"Now, we have nothing to worry about," he announced to his deputy. "Borhan has taken all the responsibility; there will be peace in Greentown very soon."

But neither the sheriff nor Borhan had noticed the man standing on the pavement keeping a close watch on them.

That evening, the man going into the *Lifeway Bank and Insurance* was Mathew Rust's foreman, Carl Weapon.

The man looked like a living skeleton.

It was quite remarkable that this bony man could manage a whole ranch. He must have been thirty or thirty five years old. His two front teeth stuck out like a rabbit's and his body was as thin as a bamboo cane. Despite his fragile appearance, however, Carl was a very cunning man. Even if his brain did not always work as it should do, he sometimes came up with some clever ideas.

Carl was not surprised to see strong security inside the bank. Armed guards were pacing up and down like soldiers. Carl went up to the counter whistling and gave the cashier a cheque. In return, he was given a wad of banknotes, which he counted carefully as he left the bank.

He looked sharply around him when he reached the road. Then he crossed over and went to an abandoned shed behind the tailor's shop. This was where "Mister" had told him to meet.

A lot of things had happened that day. Mister's work had been interrupted again and again. The day before Mister had ordered Carl to get rid of Rust's son, Vic. That was why Carl had sent Tom and Hins to the bar. The idea was that Tom and Hins would deliberately make trouble with Vic so that the fight would turn into shooting.

Carl had known Vic for a long time now. Although he carried a gun in his holster, his behaviour was worse than a drunk's. So either Tom or his brother Hins could blast off his head without difficulty. Managing the rest of it should have been as easy as pie. But nothing had gone according to plan. Vic was totally unharmed and instead both of the brothers were dead. Things could still be managed though, but if someone recognised the two dead men or found out that they were Mister's people, then it didn't bear thinking about Mister's reaction!

Carl shivered in fear for a moment. His heart was pounding with dread.

He wondered what would happen when he went

behind the tailor's shop.

Carl did not know what "Mister" was really called. Mister's own people called him "Mister", and so he did too. But it was obvious from the man's appearance and expression that he was cruel and unscrupulous. The cold eyes in his lupine face gave the impression that he had seen many deaths and was responsible for many of them too. It was evident that he would not hesitate to redden his hands in other men's blood, laughing happily.

Carl pulled himself together. He crossed the street and turned into the narrow road behind the tailor's shop.

He felt several pairs of eyes staring at him. He stopped in front of the shed. A man was leaning against a pillar in the shadows. Carl knew without any doubt that it was Mister. He looked at the man's face and relaxed slightly. A man of such power and influence wouldn't bother to make someone helpless for nothing, so there was nothing to be worried about. Mister would certainly not harm him without questioning him. Moreover, Mister would have never had any success without his advice. Thanks to Carl, Mister had set a wonderful trap to make it very easy to loot the whole town!

The plan had almost succeeded...

It wouldn't take long to loot everything.

Carl cleared his throat.

"Mister, according to your instructions I sent Tom and Hins to work. It was their own fault that they lost their lives. What can I do here?" He stopped.

There was no reply. So Carl continued. "We can forget about Vic for a few days and do something different," he suggested. "We could take Vic's father instead of Vic… that man is extremely honest, quite the opposite of his son! If we can get rid of him, then I will possess the whole ranch."

Carl waited for Mister to reply, but still no word passed his lips.

"The thing is, if we can control Mathew Rust, then we can take over almost half of the town. And it's a trifling matter to bankrupt *Triple J* ranch. We have a lot of things to sort, so if we can finish the Lifeway Bank by implementing it, everything will simply fall apart!"

At last Carl finished his speech, but there was still no reply.

Carl began to feel anxious again. He took a few

steps forward.

"What's wrong Mister?"

Then he stopped right where he was and realised that something was amiss. He had been gesticulating with his hands as he talked, but now his hands reached for his gun. Just then, the person in the shadows spoke in a thunderous voice, making Carl freeze with fear.

"Stay where you are, Carl. My people have got their guns pointing at you! It's Sheriff Dalton!"

The sheriff's huge body lumbered out of the darkness of the shed into the moonlight. Carl was more than taken aback to see him there.

"Don't be scared, Carl," said the sheriff. "Your plans are really marvellous. But right now, I want your gun belt."

Carl was totally lost for words. This time his brain failed to think up a solution. He panicked as he heard the sound of guns being cocked and began to unbuckle his gun belt.

Johnson got hold of Martin after the terrible incident in Parcy's Bar. He ignored all Martin's Excuses and took him to Jay & Jenny's restaurant for supper. He wanted to make the day a memorable one. In the end, Martin gave in to Johnson's insistence. He kept thinking about Jenny, but he had no inkling that his heart would be broken over supper.

Over the last twenty-four hours Martin had thought quite a lot about Jenny and imagined them being together, but all his dreams were shattered in an instant when Johnson, who was drinking a glass of whisky, suddenly said, "pray for me, buddy, when I become the foreman of the *Triple J* ranch and get married to Jenny…"

Afterwards, Martin could never remember how he had controlled himself. He had eaten his supper without showing any particular emotion and had managed to keep on smiling. Then he left the restaurant as quickly as possible.

On the way to his hotel room, he met a man in the corridor. He was so preoccupied with his thoughts of Jenny and Johnson that he didn't stop to wonder if he was familiar to him or not. It was only when he was closing his door that he realised that there were three people observing him closely.

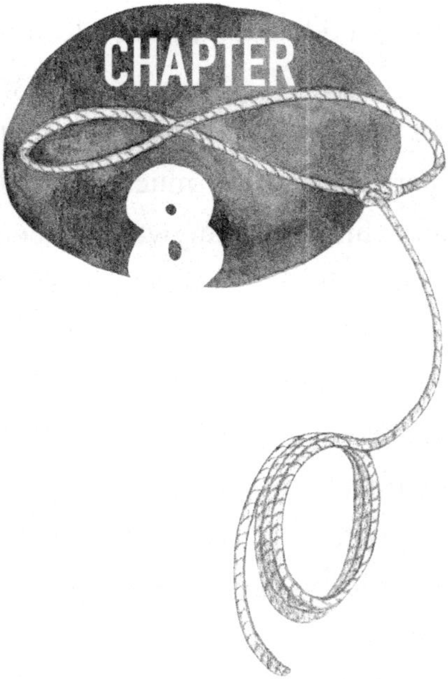

There was something preying on Borhan's mind and stopping him from going to sleep. He was lying in bed, staring at the ceiling. He knew that Martin was in the next room.

He was worried about Martin. There was no sound coming from his room, but Borhan was sufficiently acquainted with him to know that Martin never slept continuously for several hours.

It seemed odd that he was sleeping unusually soundly.

Borhan wondered if there was something wrong. Had he perhaps had too much to drink? That was very unlike him, and anyway he could hold his liquor. When Martin returned to his room, he had pretended not to recognise Borhan and his two companions in the corridor. Moreover, before Reeve and Dave left, they had knocked on his door and he hadn't answered.

Borhan felt there was something wrong. He knew that Martin had had supper with Johnson earlier that evening.

Wait a second…

What if one of his enemies had mixed some sleeping pills with his meal? And if that were the case, then the enemy in question would have only one reason for doing so.

They would want to kill Martin while he slept!

The reason was very clear now.

Borhan got out of bed quietly, so as not to arouse anybody.

He took his six-gun and a packet of poisonous Oxious dust powder from under the pillow.

Oxious powder was very effective for neutering

an enemy. First it suffocated them and then, after a certain time, it would make them blind.

Borhan put the six-gun inside his trousers.

The room was lit slightly by the moonlight, which was filtering through the windows and making it possible to see everything in the room.

Borhan approached the door stealthily.

He could hear the sound of footsteps in the corridor. It sounded as if the person was walking on tiptoe and this made him suspicious. If it were someone from one of the other rooms or a boarder, then there was no need to tiptoe. Perhaps the person had a special reason for walking so quietly. Perhaps the reason that Borhan had thought about a while ago was true!

Death itself was coming to kill Martin!

Saliman's hotel was very quiet at night. Everything was abnormally silent. The glow of the lamps hanging here and there along the corridor created an atmosphere of fear.

The stranger was advancing slowly but surely towards room number 14. Everything was quiet.

All the people in the hotel were sleeping soundly.

The man was holding a sharp dagger very tightly in one hand. He had no other weapons. The last lamp hanging from the corridor wall spluttered and died, plunging everything into darkness.

The man was thinking hard about the situation. He knew he could just as easily go back the way he had come. There was no need to take any extra precautions. The victim was already a dead body; just the soul still had to fly away.

"Mister" had told him not to try and do anything courageous, but just to dispose of the person who was causing so many problems. Although it might seem cowardly, the stranger knew very well that it would be impossible to overcome Martin while he was still awake. So nobody wanted to take the risk of disposing with Martin except Mister, and nobody wanted to kill him like a coward either. It was probable that he would sleep all through the next day and night.

The stranger smiled to himself. After a while he found himself standing before the door of room 14. The corridor was plunged in darkness; only a feeble ray of moonlight was illuminating it. The stranger looked swiftly and carefully up and down the corridor. Everything seemed alright. Since it was likely that he would have to run away quickly, he had come barefoot. Still he couldn't dissimulate the occasional creaking of the wooden floorboards. He hoped that the noise would not wake anyone up. The assassin touched the doorknob cautiously. He knew that in somnolent state, Martin would have forgotten to lock the door. He turned the knob slowly and the door opened, proving the stranger absolutely right!

About half an hour later, the moon had disappeared below the horizon and in the darkness of the night no sound could be heard – not a single cricket or the barking of a dog.

"So, Mr. Simpson, I'll give you one more chance to answer my questions," Borhan said to the man sitting on the chair in front of him. The man was dressed only in his underwear and was sweating like a breathless person.

"I-I'm really telling you the truth Sir, believe me!" the man called Simpson stammered.

"You want me to believe me that you were going to the toilet in the middle of the night with a dangerous dagger in your hand?" Borhan asked, waving his six-gun under his nose.

"Ac-actually, not exactly that, Sir. I was going to the toilet alright but I had been thinking of stealing..."

"Why did you choose this room?" Borhan asked in an ice-cold voice.

"How can I convince you Sir? I-I am..." Simpson stopped as he saw Borhan getting up from his chair.

Borhan slapped Simpson hard across the cheek. He pointed at Martin's sleeping body.

"He's my friend," he said. "If I wake him up now and tell him everything that happened, I don't think you'll need to worry about me anymore. So what do you say?"

There were no lights inside the room, but Borhan could make out the man's eyes in the dim moonlight and see that they expressed pure panic. Simpson wiped the sweat from his forehead. It seemed as if he could not decide what to do next. He looked like a restless chimpanzee trapped in a cage.

"So what I'm telling you," Borhan said again, "is that if you can answer my questions properly, then I'll give you the opportunity to escape before this man wakes up. If you want, I won't even mention tonight's incidents."

Simpson thought for a minute. Then he said slowly, "Alright, Sir, tell me what you want to know."

"Yeah, now you're talking sense. But remember – if you try and tell a single lie then I'll cut you into pieces. It's up to you."

Simpson couldn't utter a word and he began to tremble. The man standing in front of him would definitely keep his word – that much was obvious.

"So tell me – who sent you?"

"Mister sent me."

"Mister, who the hell is that?"

"We all call him that."

"Carl, Rust's foreman - does he have anything to do with him?"

"I think they have quite a close relationship, but in front of us other guys, they talk to each other like they were strangers."

"Does he come from Greentown like Carl?"

"Yes, I think so, but I can't say for sure. He always wears a mask in front of us. I've never seen his face."

"I've never seen your face in this town either!"

"Mister hired about five people like me from

elsewhere."

"And how many people does he have in all?"

"There must be at least ten people."

"Did he do all the rustling and bank robberies with so few people?"

Simpson did not reply.

Borhan wanted to be sure he was telling the truth.

"But Simpson, where does Mister put all the cattle?"

"They're smuggled to the North in the same round-up and the rancher is told that there is some mistake in the headcount."

"So I guess Carl helps him, doesn't he? That's how thousands of animals could simply disappear under our very noses!"

Borhan was astonished by the procedure. "But Simpson, it's not possible for him to do all that alone – how does he manage for the other ranches?"

"I don't know, I can't really explain."

"Well, explain as well as you can, Simpson."

"As far as I can guess, someone from the *Triple J* ranch must be involved with Carl. But did you know that Carl was captured by the sheriff tonight?"

"Is that so? Very good, that makes things easier for me. Well, let me ask you one last question - where can I find Mister's gang?"

"If we don't have any assignment, we take cover during the day. But at night, we go to Matthew Rust's ranch. Carl hides us in the bunkhouses and we leave at daybreak."

"Where do you take cover?"

"You know the Pine Tree lake? In the forest there."

"Hm..." Borhan fell silent. He looked at the sleeping figure of Martin and then again at Simpson. He could clearly hear Simpson gulping. The poor man had talked continuously up to then.

"If you don't go back, what will Mister think of you?"

Simpson was scared now.

He shifted uncomfortably in his chair.

"You-you told me that you would let me go Sir..."

"Why are you so scared? I only want to know whether Mister will go for another plan if you don't kill Martin."

"I-I can't say, Sir. B-but Sir, I can't go back.

Mister will kill me!"

"OK." Borhan sat on the bed again. "Take your clothes."

"Wi-will you let me go, Sir?" Simpson seemed to hesitate.

"Don't you believe me? Then do this – write a letter to Mister so that he thinks that you were too cowardly to kill Martin and that you're leaving town because you're scared of Mister. Is that OK?"

For the first time, Borhan saw hope in Simpson's eyes, as if he had escaped from death. His pale face came back to life again as he recovered from his fright.

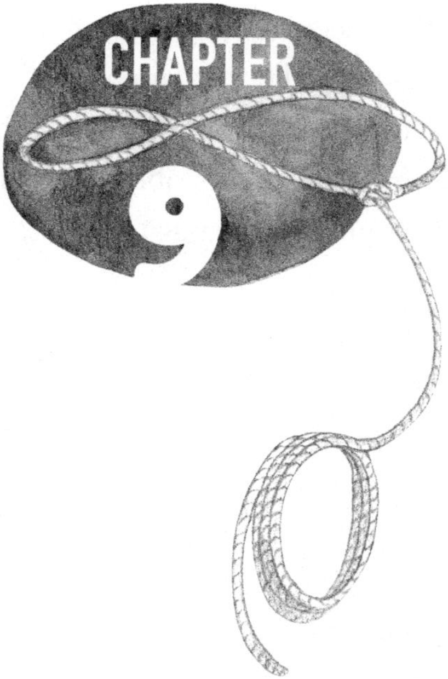

One of the gang member told the others, "Mister has informed us that Carl might speak out at any time."

"But Mister will say goodbye as soon as he's paid us, so we don't need to worry too much about that now."

"Yes, but that's not the main issue. Don't forget that Simpson is missing. We don't even know if he accomplished the work he was sent out for. I think

Simpson has been captured and that's why Mister doesn't want to take any more risks. Once we've left, he'll escape as well. Moreover, if Carl blabs out everything he knows about Mister, then we'll be finished too. So we must get away as soon as possible and be careful not to leave any tracks."

"OK, but Mister was supposed to meet us today. The sun will be up in only a couple of hours and people will be about, which will be dangerous for us."

"Don't worry, I think we're safe here. If Carl tells the sheriff about us, then the poor guy will most probably look for us on the other side of the lake and he won't find us there."

"Then…." The man stopped talking.

Someone was knocking at the door. All eyes were immediately riveted on the door.

One of the rustlers went cautiously to the door, his pistol at the ready. "Who is it? David?" Then the rustler pronounced the code.

"No, it's the hostler."

The rustler pulled the door slightly ajar and observed the person behind it. He was certain that it was their man and he reassured the rest of the gang.

Everybody put their guns back into their holsters

and relaxed.

As they sat there nonchalantly, the masked person quickly entered the room.

Just thirty seconds later they realised with shock that they had made a terrible mistake!

They remained glued to their seats as it was too late to react.

A group of gunmen burst into the room, pointing their firearms at the group.

There was no doubt about the stranger's identity - when the man removed his mask, everybody recognised the sheriff.

"Don't be surprised, my friends. I'm the one who brought you here disguised as your Mister. And you have all proved what you deserve by easily falling into my trap. Now, everybody surrender your pistols to my men and come with us like good boys. And don't forget that in the meantime, Mister is preparing more people to kill you guys because we deliberately informed him that we had captured you. He can kill you anytime he wants, for fear that you may inform us about his whereabouts."

There were muffled protests among the rustlers.

"Silence!" the sheriff roared and everybody

immediately froze.

"Go and release Mr. Rust's son Vic and send him back to their ranch," the sheriff ordered an armed man beside him. "I'm going to take all this vermin to jail. We'll see who can save Mister from me now!"

The mistress of the *Triple J* ranch, Mrs. Jerri, was pacing impatiently up and down her room. Her face showed a great deal of worry and uncertainty.

Jan was sitting on a chair, rubbing his hands together nervously, and Jenny was standing close by him.

It was well past midnight. It was so quiet you could hear a pin drop. It would soon be another day.

In the room next door, Vic's father, Mr. Rust, was talking with Mr. Jerri. Robertson was there too, leaning against the wall. His son, Johnson, was outside with the ranch crews, who were impatiently waiting with firearms for what was bound to come. At any moment they might be attacked.

"I've made a terrible mistake. All this time I've been sleeping with the enemy, it's ridiculous!" Mr. Rust said in dismay.

"Calm yourself Mathew. Carl will be punished

the way he deserves. Let them catch Mister first." Jerri said quietly.

"I've heard that Borhan came to town." Robertson continued. "Now only God knows what will happen!"

"I don't know why, but I have a feeling that Borhan is not involved in any of this," Mathew Rust said. "If he was, then somehow or another I would surely have seen his gang on my ranch. I know every single member of my crew personally, and when I recruited them Carl hadn't yet arrived. You may not know, Jerri, but I brought Carl with me from another place."

"Still, you shouldn't stay alone on your ranch. It's good that you came to me. If your crews are alright, then your ranch will be alright too."

"I'm rather worried about Vic. I spoke to the sheriff. He was supposed to release Vic, but…."

"Don't worry, I sent one of my men with a letter. He's bound to return with Vic."

"But whatever you say, the sheriff will get every bit of information out of Carl. What a strange name for their boss, *Mister!* Hah!!"

"I think that Carl was going to give plans to Mister to murder you. In that case, I don't think they would spare me either. But even if the sheriff can capture the gang, can he capture Mister too?"

Robertson shook his head. "That brat Mister is surely planning something in secret! He may come and create chaos at any moment."

"You're quite right, Robert. We shouldn't be sitting idle like this. We should help the sheriff…."

"Someone's coming!" Johnson called from outside.

"Maybe it's your son…." Jerri smiled wryly at Mathew Rust, then he ordered sharply, "let him come, it may be Vic!"

Robertson left the room. After a minute or two Vic staggered in with him. They were all shocked to see the state he was in and they ran to hold him up. There was blood all over his body and it was obvious from his face that he had been brutally tortured. His clothes were in shreds.

"The deputy sheriff was going to take him back to the ranch, but on the way they met with our ranch men.There was a big misunderstanding and some shooting. The deputy sheriff and Vic were shot but our crew managed to get them back here safely."

"What? Where did you leave the deputy?" Jerri

asked impatiently.

"In the bunkhouse with our crews."

Mrs. Jerri now came into the room and Mathew and Jerri left Vic in her capable hands before going out to the bunkhouse.

The deputy sheriff had been badly shot. He was seriously wounded and was fighting with death.

Johnson sat beside him, looking perturbed. When he saw Jerri, he said, "Uncle, this man is trying to say something, but I can't understand him."

Jerri bent down and put his ear close to the man's lips to try and make out what he was saying. The man was whispering with difficulty and his voice was unclear, but the little that Jerri managed to catch made the expression on his face change radically. It was one of complete stupefaction.

Nobody knew what was going on and everyone was staring at Jerri as he stood up slowly.

"Nobody tells a lie before they die," he said. "Quickly send for a doctor and a priest and, Robert, tell the armed forces to be ready immediately. We have to go to town." Then Jerri left the room. Everybody watched him leave with astonishment!

#

It had been a while since the Simpson guy had been sent away. In the meantime, Reeve and Dave had been brought from the hotel, holding naked six-guns.

Borhan was sitting in Martin's room. The latter had eventually woken up, though not without difficulty. Now he was pacing up and down the room.

"You've done a very strange thing!" Borhan remarked, breaking the silence.

Martin stopped walking and stood in front of him.

Then he gave him a sharp glance. "Well you could have warned me, couldn't you?"

"Yes I could, but I didn't know about these girly issues…"

"Look Borhan, stop your silly talk!" Martin stood up straight. He lit a cigar with Dave's help.

Borhan gave him time. "OK, now listen," he said to Martin, "We have some important information. You can be sure that there will be no lack of evidence. You are saved and that is the main thing. Now, please prepare yourself mentally."

Martin nodded at him.

He pointed at his pistol and asked to have it back.

Borhan handed it to him, he put it in his holster and in exchange gave Borhan his cigar.

"I'm ready. Do we start now?"

"Yes," Borhan replied, drawing on the cigar. "But remember, we have to catch Mister alive."

"There will be no harm done to him. What about you?"

"We have our men at the *Triple J* ranch. Though ironically, Simpson…"

"Simpson…?"

"That rustler, just a while ago who was… well, if he was telling us the truth, then there may be a bit of a fight. But it shouldn't spread to the house."

"What about Carl?"

"I guess he's dead by now. But Vic has been released," Reeve announced, nonchalantly. "I saw him a little while ago…."

"Wait a minute!" Martin exclaimed. "Vic has been released and in the meantime Carl is dead… What are you telling me?"

"It's quite simple," Borhan replied. "Carl was poisoned with his dinner, because Mister had to do something that the townsfolk could believe in order to shut him up. At the same time, he has probably planned something for his own gang so that he can hide somewhere. It's certain that he suspects us because he knows very well that we will have recognised him by now. He thinks we don't have any proof against him, and so we want to catch his companions. So he…"

"So if he thinks that, he would deliberately kill his companions." Martin interrupted Borhan, "If we can't capture his men, then we won't be able to capture him either, am I right?"

"Absolutely. And he must be putting these ideas into action somewhere right now!"

"Then let's go immediately, we mustn't waste any more time." Martin headed towards the door. Just then they heard the townspeople cheering. The noise penetrated the silence of the night. There were some sounds of shooting too.

"So the game has begun," Dave murmured.

CHAPTER 10

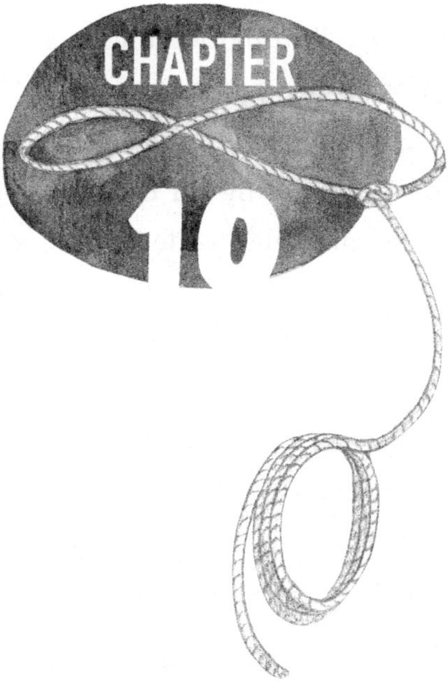

There was a large crowd in front of the sheriff's office.

Everyone was shouting excitedly. Only a few minutes before they had been sleeping soundly, but now they were calling out impatiently to learn more.

The moonlight penetrated the darkness of the night, clearly illuminating everything all around.

"Dear friends!" the sheriff addressed the

townsfolk, "we are finally going to succeed after all our attempts. It has taken some time, but we have now successfully captured the rustlers who were responsible for creating all the unrest in town. We still need to catch the leader of the gang, but I'm sure if you help us, that shouldn't take too long."

"We're ready and willing to help!" many of the onlookers called out.

"Thank you. You all know that these people have been making trouble in town in many ways, robbing the bank and cattle rustling… What do you think would be proper punishment for them?"

"Hang them all!" somebody proposed vociferously.

"Let them bathe in their own blood!" others shouted.

The sheriff raised his hand to stop them, "Your wish will be granted. But before that, help me find the person who is behind all this. Help me get the information out of them!"

"Your wish will be granted as well!" the people promised.

"Then wait until dawn. In the meantime, I'll find a way to capture the gang leader by interrogating his men."

The sheriff went back into his office, satisfied with the townspeople's reaction.

The crowd gradually broke up and people started to return home. The sheriff's deputies remained near the jailhouse, guarding it with their guns.

Martin and Borhan watched everything from afar and were reassured by the way the sheriff was managing the situation. Even so, they knew that he was taking a risk by putting Mister's people behind bars.

They went to the office.

The sheriff looked up when he heard the door opening. He smiled while he saw Borhan entering the office, but was surprised to see Martin with him.

"Hey Borhan, come along! I was waiting for you, I knew you'd come."

They looked at the scared faces of the prisoners. There were about ten of them. But their eyes soon became riveted on a dead body on the floor, covered with a white sheet.

It must be Carl's corpse.

"Sit down," the sheriff invited. "There's nothing new to tell. You can see with your own eyes." The sheriff gestured towards the prisoners.

"Yes, it's all obvious. But how did it happen… and this dead body…?" Borhan surveyed and asked.

"That's Carl. He was the one who informed me about their hiding place and who gave me Mister's description. I tricked them into coming to town and then captured them. On the way back, I saw that Carl had been poisoned…" The sheriff paused. "I found a dead body in the meadows - it was my deputy. I had ordered him to release Vic from jail, so I'm not sure what happened."

"I understand. But what are you doing about the real criminal?" Borhan wanted to know.

"First have a look to see if there is anyone on your list as well. Here, do it quickly!" Sheriff handed him the list.

Everyone turned towards the door as one of the guards came in.

"Sir, a group of riders are heading this way," he announced. "What should we do?"

"Let them come and don't create any trouble," the sheriff replied. "But keep a close eye on them, so that they can't come in here with weapons."

The deputy left to carry out the orders. The

sheriff smiled at Borhan and Martin. "We'd better be careful. Who knows, maybe the stranger really is this 'Mister'."

They all remained silent.

All of sudden, some shots rang out.

Reeve and Dave emerged stealthily from the dark bushes around the jailhouse. Something was flashing in the moonlight.

Razor blades!

They parted ways to approach their victims from two different angles, like reapers.

Dave was able to fell a man at his very first attempt and a second man was swiftly brought to the ground by Reeve. There had been two other men standing by the jailhouse window; they had both been silenced as well. Reeve's and Dave's hands were red with blood.

They wiped their hands with their handkerchiefs.

The razor blade had done its gory work.

Their pistols were at the ready as they waited for the signal.

There were four more soldiers in front of the jailhouse who had to be dealt with. As Reeve and Dave waited for the signal, a volley of shots penetrated the silence of the night! Immediately afterwards, Reeve fell to the ground with a large hole in his head. Dave was startled, but quickly threw himself to the ground to protect himself.

A bullet whistled over his head and he responded right away with a bullet of his own. The bullets were coming from the front side of the jail.

Suddenly the shooting stopped and was replaced by the sound of horse's hooves. Dave prepared himself. He took the pistol that had fallen from Reeve's hand and started crawling to a safer place where he could take cover.

But in the end he could not save himself....

He had run out of ammunition.

"Put your hands up!" the sheriff ordered in a calm but firm voice.

He was pointing his gun at Martin and Borhan.

They remained speechless.

Shortly before, the gang of rustlers had been in prison, but now they were all outside with guns in their hands.

The sheriff ordered two of them to search Martin and Borhan, but they found nothing in particular.

The sheriff seemed surprised.

"What's wrong my friends, how come you're going round without any weapons?"

Borhan smiled. "Yeah, I suppose it was rather foolish of us!"

The sheriff raised his eyebrows.

"Don't you think you were a little too foolhardy? If you really knew who I was, then why did you come deliberately into the lion's den?"

"Maybe we wouldn't have come if we had known that you would show your real face so quickly," Martin replied.

There was no more shooting.

The sheriff looked at his men.

"My friends," he said, "we need to help our people outside. Go and fetch them and tell them that the gunfight has been postponed. I have something to do first."

Some of the rustlers left to obey his orders.

The sheriff looked at Martin and Borhan again.

"What do you have in mind, sheriff?" Borhan asked him.

"Right now I want to kill you two!" the sheriff said, with his hand on the trigger.

"Hey wait a minute! Why are you acting so quickly? There are still things we want to know!"

"I'm not going to waste my time answering your silly questions!"

"Well that's strange! If you already knew that we suspected you, then you could have finished us a long time ago without wasting your valuable time, sheriff!"

"That's right, but I needed you."

"What do you mean?"

"I've used you for my own ends. You couldn't possibly guess that. I allowed Borhan to stay in town, and you, Martin, I introduced you to the townspeople in such a way that they all suspect you to be a bounty hunter who came here in search of a terrible criminal. Of course, the reason is almost true for you, although without your bounty hunter identity. I know very well that you are really U.S. Marshal Harry Laslore!"

"Very strange!" Martin was really surprised. "But what could you accomplish with all this?"

Borhan intervened. "He used his own people to make trouble and then blamed and captured my people instead. Rustling, bank robbery – he did all that just to make people think that someone was trying to destroy Greentown. At the same time, he pretended to be an honest and just person by staging their arrest!"

"You're absolutely right!" There was an evil smile on the sheriff's face. "But to be honest, Martin - sorry, Harry - wasn't expected here at all. His arrival thwarted my plans. But I didn't know that he had been brought here by you, Borhan. I only realised that when you told me that you were staying at Saliman's hotel. So I sent a man to put some poison pills in his supper which could kill him. I guessed that if you really had any connection with Harry then you would try and save him, and things went just as I expected. Because of that, I realised that you must suspect that I would kill my own people to save myself."

"But why did you kill Carl?"

"I had to get rid of him one way or another because sometimes I spoke to him without my mask. He was the only one who could identify me. Also, it was due to his carelessness that you came here. Tell me, Borhan," the sheriff continued, "why did you bring Martin to Greentown? Was it because of the unrest?"

"No. I found out that you had been in another town in the West before coming here, but your movements or location couldn't be traced. That's why I brought Harry here, so that he could observe each and every individual in the town and see if anyone had a criminal background. As a matter of fact, Harry identified you on the very first day; he told me that you used to kill people for money. From then on, I knew that people had made a terrible mistake by putting you in a position of authority, to protect the town, when you were actually the one responsible for destroying everything."

"Hahaha!" The sheriff laughed loudly and rather manically. "The protector is the one who destroys! Hahaha!!"

"You've laughed enough, Dalton!" expostulated Borhan with disgust. "I was an outlaw once too. I've killed dozens of people when necessary. But I've never seen a brat like you!"

"You never saw one before, but you've seen one now!" Martin alias Harry Laslore exclaimed. "Forget it, Borhan, we got our answers. Dalton, you can shoot us now without another thought!"

Sheriff Dalton never imagined that Harry would say such a thing. The smile was wiped off his face. He clenched his pistol and looked at them suspiciously.

"Wait a minute! I think I may have understood something… It's not possible that wild wolves like you can surrender so easily to their fate." Dalton stood up slowly. "…which can only mean that the people my men were fighting were actually your men? But… but what about the men that I ordered to attack you here?"

"What do you mean?" Harry and Borhan said together.

"I knew that you two would come here. So I told them to come and attack you. I would...."

"You would wound us and disguise us as 'Mister' so that you could implement your plan," Martin interrupted him. "Your strategies are fantastic, Dalton, I'm very impressed!" Martin said, although his tone sounded more insulting than impressed. Ignoring Dalton's gun, he stood up and looked the "Sheriff" straight in the eye. "But now the game's over!"

Dalton didn't have the time to press the trigger. Martin alias Harry pressed a handful of strychnine powder on his face. At the same time, he scattered more strychnine powder that he had dissimulated in his boots over the startled rustlers. He had kept Dalton busy talking, while he quietly removed his boots. In just a couple of minutes everyone was motionless. They had all crashed to the ground, struggled feebly, and then lost consciousness. Harry and Borhan had to hold their breath so as not to inhale the powder, but they soon breathed a sigh of relief and looked at each other with satisfaction.

There was a huge crowd in front of the jailhouse. Altogether there were twelve dead bodies on the premises. In the middle of all the chaos, Borhan was weeping silently over the bodies of Dave and Reeve. The undertaker had been called to remove the corpses while the town authorities took the unconscious criminals to be imprisoned. Word soon got around that Martin Laslore was in fact U.S. Marshal Harry Laslore.

Harry wasn't interested. He had started out towards the *Triple J* ranch.

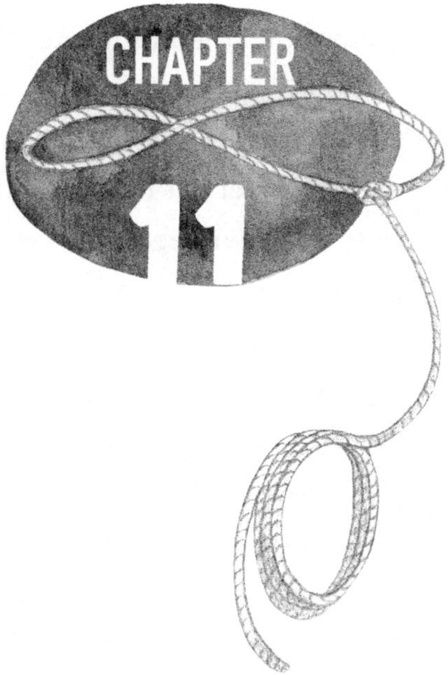

"You shouldn't take the risk, Jerri. There might be ambushers lying in wait." Mathew Rust was sitting beside the unconscious and wounded Vic.

"I'll leave Johnson to protect you," Mr. Jerri said as he checked his gun belt. "You can go with your son."

Then he murmured to himself, "That brat is trying to take over everything himself. He wants to be the king alone! I'm going to put an end to that today!"

"I can't believe that the person we gave the responsibility to protect our town is actually the one who…" Jenny made a regretful sound. She was sitting beside her mother. "And we all trusted him like fools!"

The door opened and Robertson appeared, looking agitated.

"Jerri! A gang is hiding around the ranch. They've killed two of our men!"

Robertson was shocked. As soon as he stopped talking, there was a sound of shooting outside.

"You all stay here. Don't go outside, I'm going to see what's going on," said Jerri, going into the next room with Robertson.

Two of the trustworthy crews were standing outside with their firearms. The window panes had been shattered by the assailants and the crews were responding.

"Where's Johnson?" Jerri asked.

"In the bunk house. They have no more bullets left. And we couldn't go to the cartridge room either. There were some traitors among our men."

"What?" Jerri said in despair.

"Yes, it looks like there were five of them."

There were no lights on in the room, but in the moonlight Jerri suddenly caught sight of a shadow, which quickly hid on the other side of the lake. Another shadow came out of the bunk house, but was quickly felled. That meant that Johnson and the others were trapped there.

"Robert, we can't stay here like this any longer," Jerri said. "We won't survive. There are no more bullets left in the six-guns; we must decide what to do very quickly."

The two crews were shooting at intervals. Robert told them to stop. He was thinking fast.

Jerri stood by the window to give him time to think up a plan.

He looked outside to try and assess the situation.

The shooting had stopped and there was no other noise from outside. Suddenly there was a moving shadow and a loud scream.

"Come out with your hands up, or else…."

Another shot was fired and Jerri saw that shadow had fallen to the ground. People were running towards the ranch house. Before Jerri could fire at them, they fell to the ground under another shower of bullets. At the same time, the bunkhouse door was flung open and Johnson and the other men appeared.

Jerri and Robertson could see someone else approaching from the very spot where the assailants were hiding. The moonlight lit his face. It was Martin Laslore!

Two days later in Greentown, there was great rejoicing. Once a dangerous outlaw, Borhan, was now elected as sheriff with an overwhelming majority of votes. To celebrate, there was a reception in the Town Hall. Harry Laslore was sitting beside Borhan on the stage.

A few rows ahead, Jenny was sitting on the guest seat and busy talking with other girls. Johnson could be seen with some other guys on the other side.

Borhan and Harry both saw that Jenny and Johnson were speaking to each other with their eyes.

"They're looking great, aren't they?" Martin alias Harry commented with a smile. Borhan smiled back, but did not reply.

"It's a shame I can't be present at their wedding," Harry continued, raising his glass of champagne as a toast to the happy couple. Just then Harry felt Jenny's eyes on him. He looked back at her, a little ruefully.

Harry had to return to California to start a new life. He would probably have to visit other places like Greentown. And maybe someone like Jenny would be waiting for him there.

Maybe.

———

Also by ***Uncle Nafee***

- A Secret Behind The Bungalow

CUP OF TEA. STUDIO